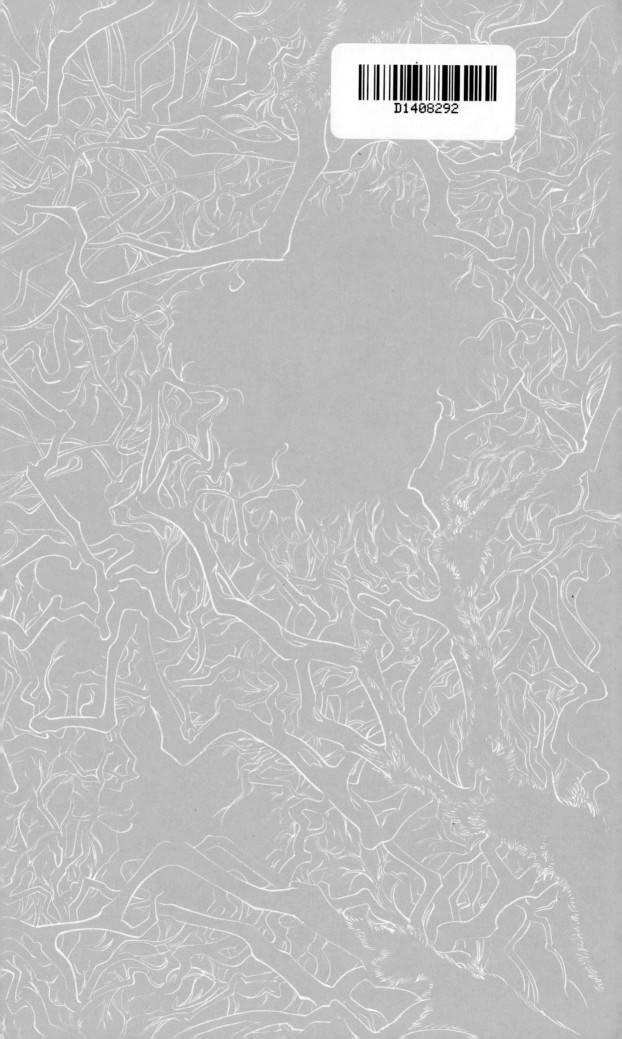

I.D.

Emma Ríos

WHY DON'T YOU LIKE YOUR BODY?

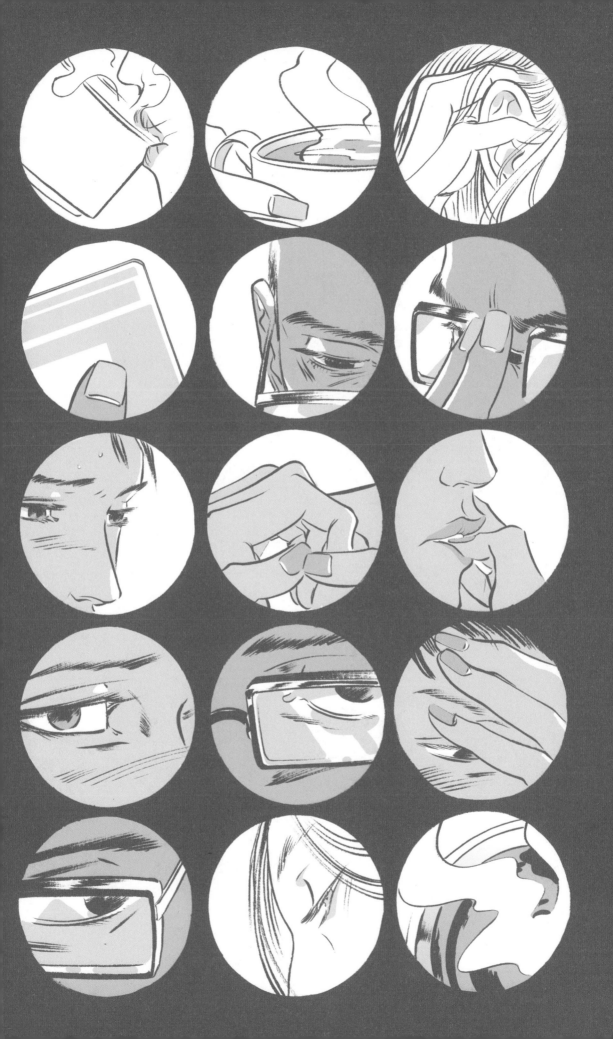

Chapter 1: Coffee, Tea, Water.

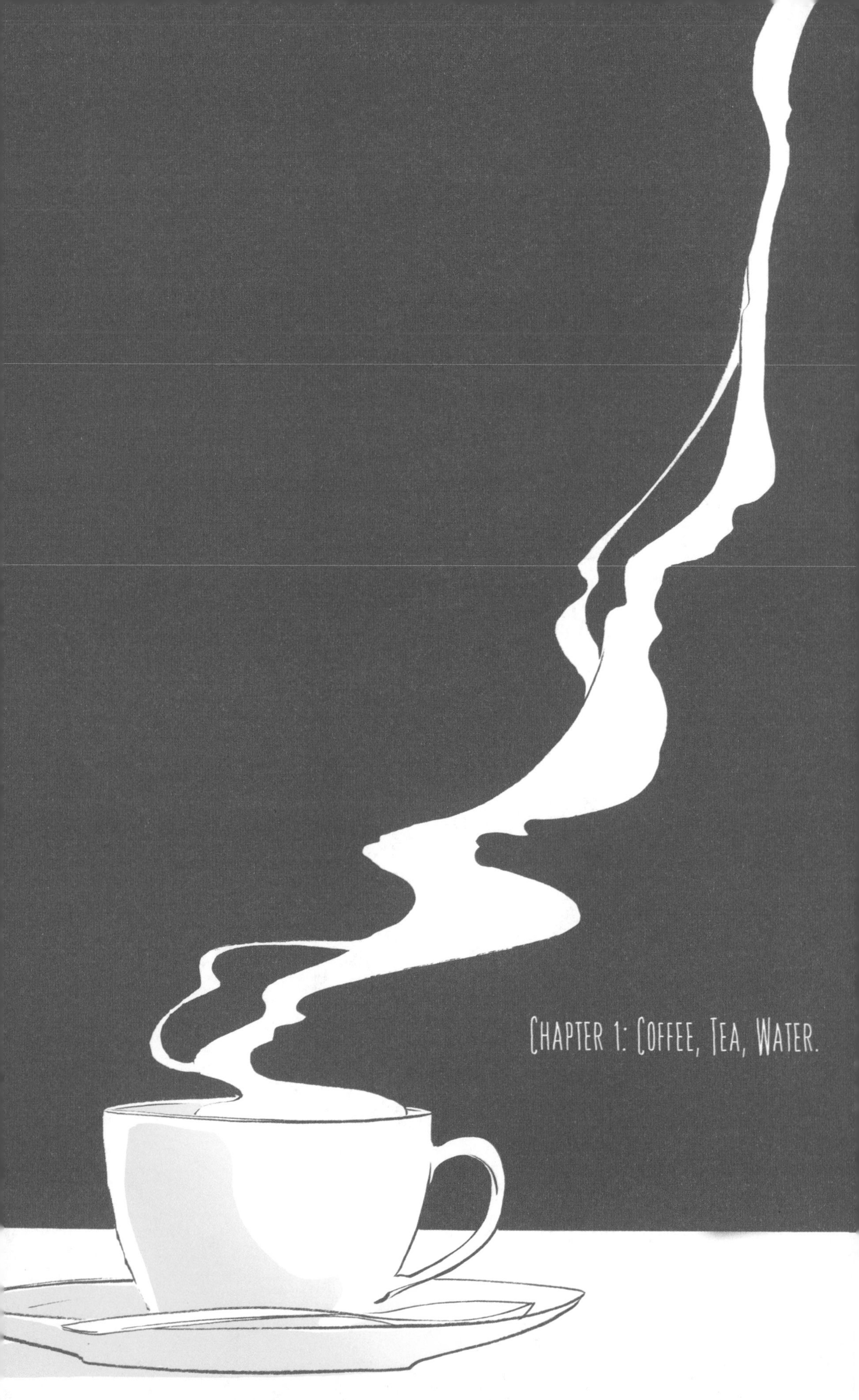

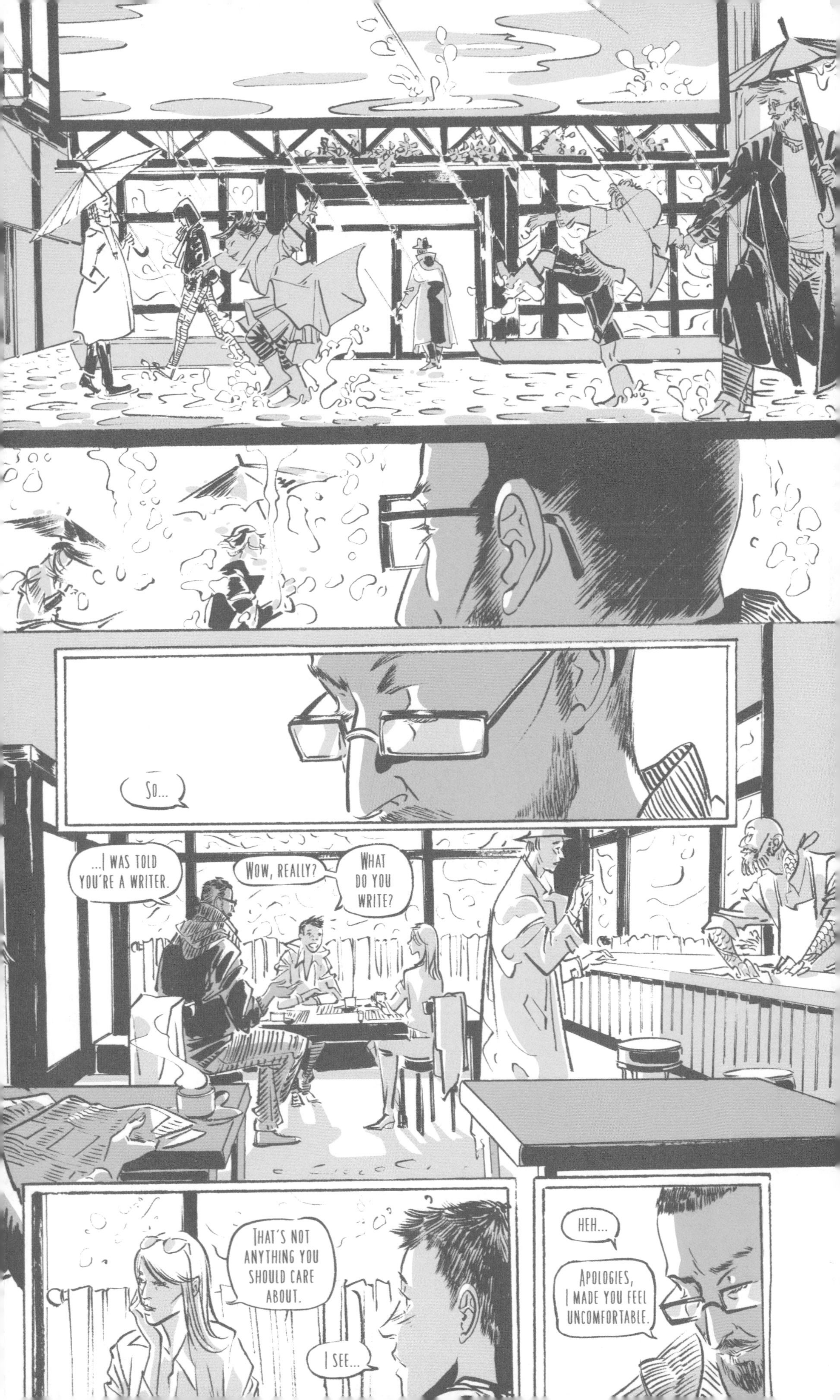

SO...
...I WAS TOLD YOU'RE A WRITER.
WOW, REALLY?
WHAT DO YOU WRITE?
THAT'S NOT ANYTHING YOU SHOULD CARE ABOUT.
I SEE...
HEH...
APOLOGIES, I MADE YOU FEEL UNCOMFORTABLE.

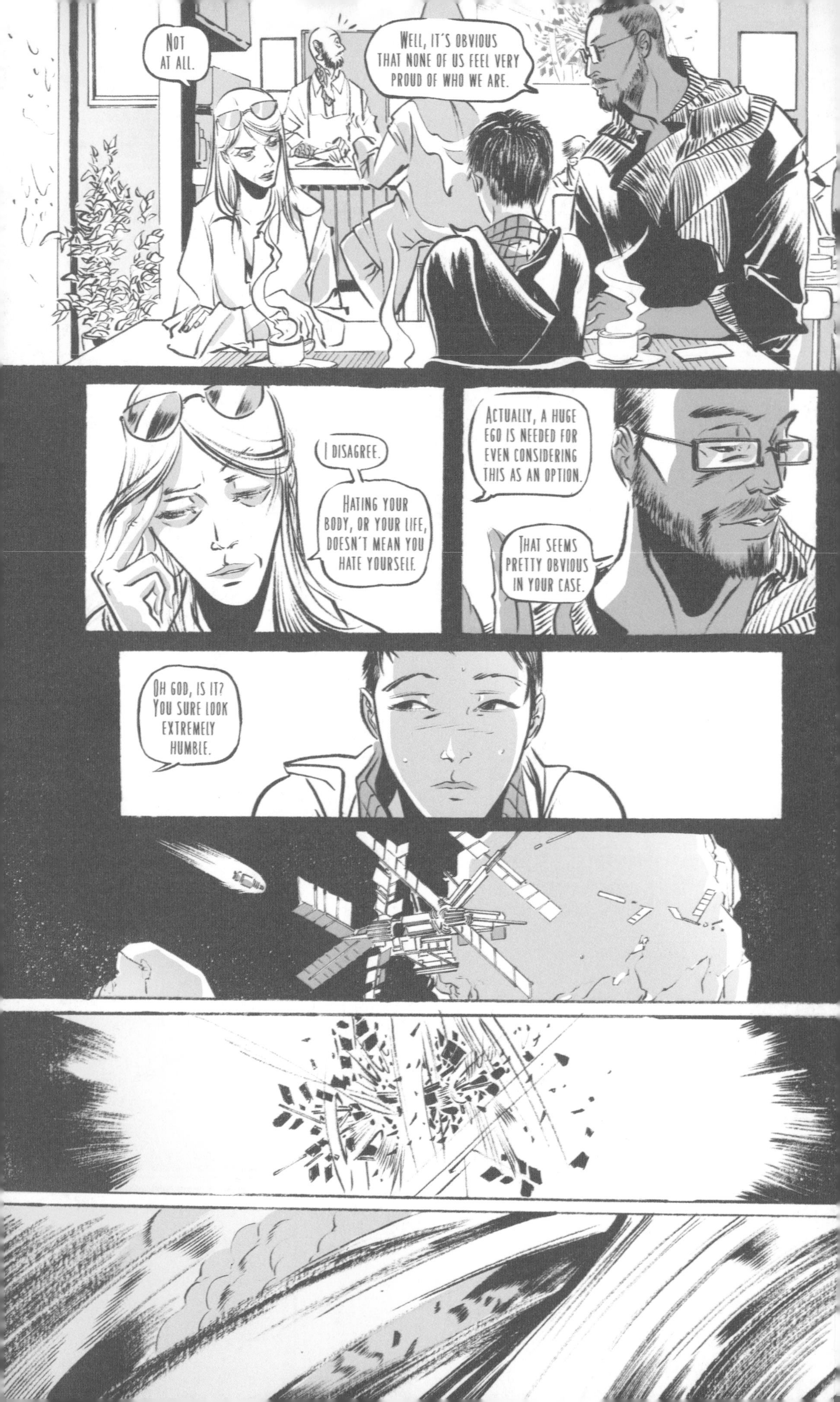
Not at all.
Well, it's obvious that none of us feel very proud of who we are.
I disagree.
Hating your body, or your life, doesn't mean you hate yourself.
Actually, a huge ego is needed for even considering this as an option.
That seems pretty obvious in your case.
Oh god, is it? You sure look extremely humble.

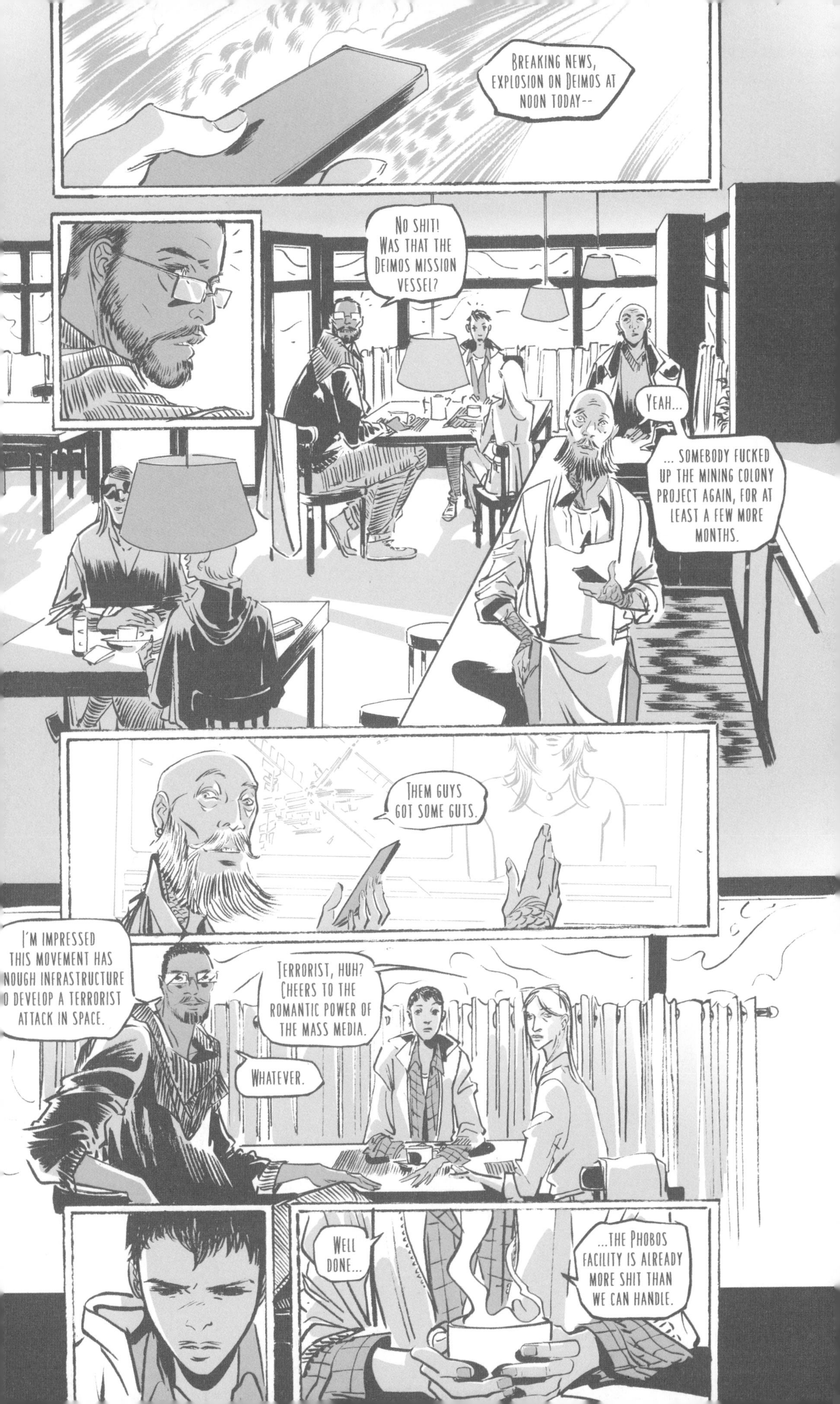

BREAKING NEWS, EXPLOSION ON DEIMOS AT NOON TODAY--
NO SHIT! WAS THAT THE DEIMOS MISSION VESSEL?
YEAH...
... SOMEBODY FUCKED UP THE MINING COLONY PROJECT AGAIN, FOR AT LEAST A FEW MORE MONTHS.
THEM GUYS GOT SOME GUTS.
I'M IMPRESSED THIS MOVEMENT HAS NOUGH INFRASTRUCTURE O DEVELOP A TERRORIST ATTACK IN SPACE.
TERRORIST, HUH? CHEERS TO THE ROMANTIC POWER OF THE MASS MEDIA.
WHATEVER.
WELL DONE...
...THE PHOBOS FACILITY IS ALREADY MORE SHIT THAN WE CAN HANDLE.

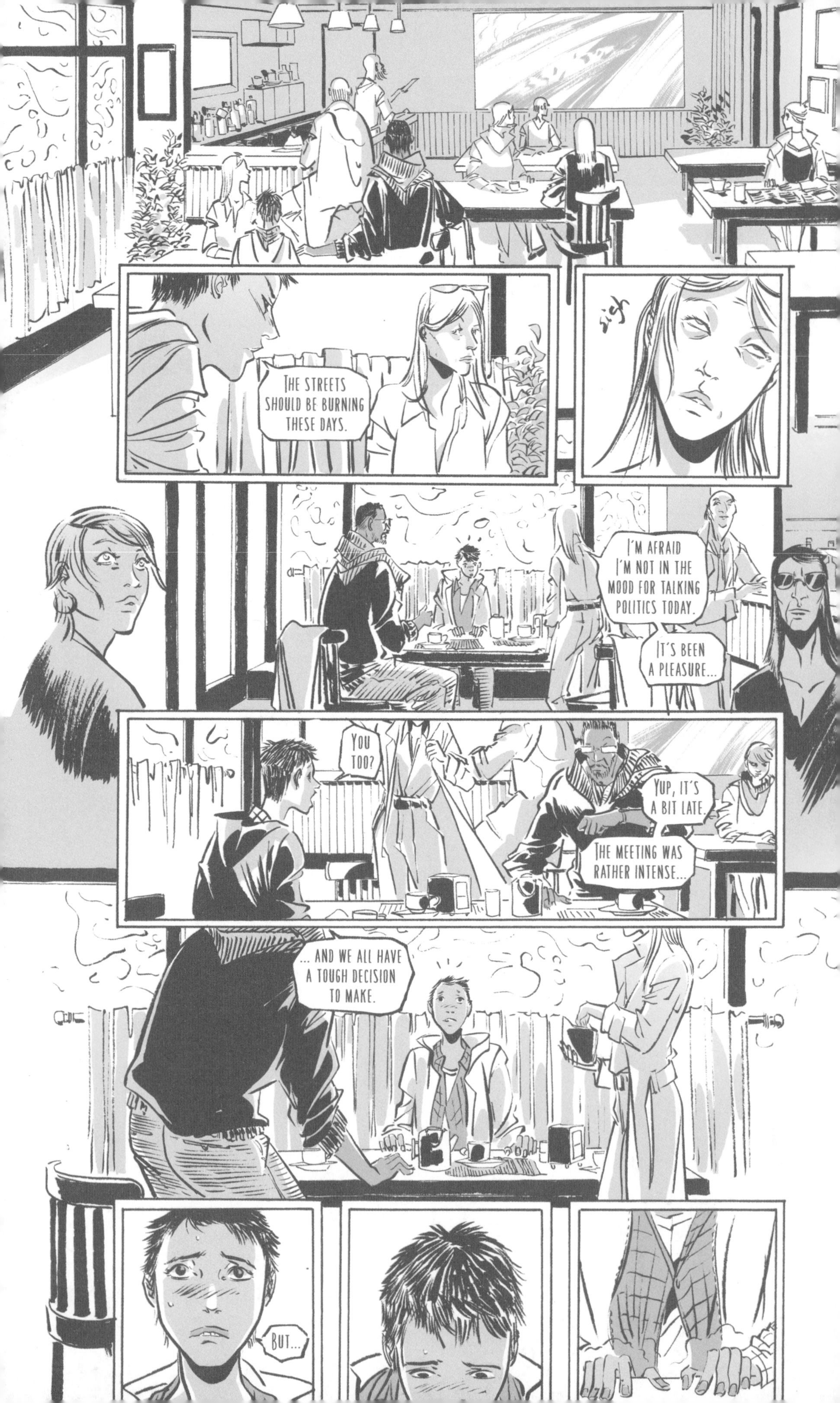

THE STREETS SHOULD BE BURNING THESE DAYS.
SIGH
I'M AFRAID I'M NOT IN THE MOOD FOR TALKING POLITICS TODAY.
IT'S BEEN A PLEASURE...
YOU TOO?
YUP, IT'S A BIT LATE.
THE MEETING WAS RATHER INTENSE...
... AND WE ALL HAVE A TOUGH DECISION TO MAKE.
BUT...

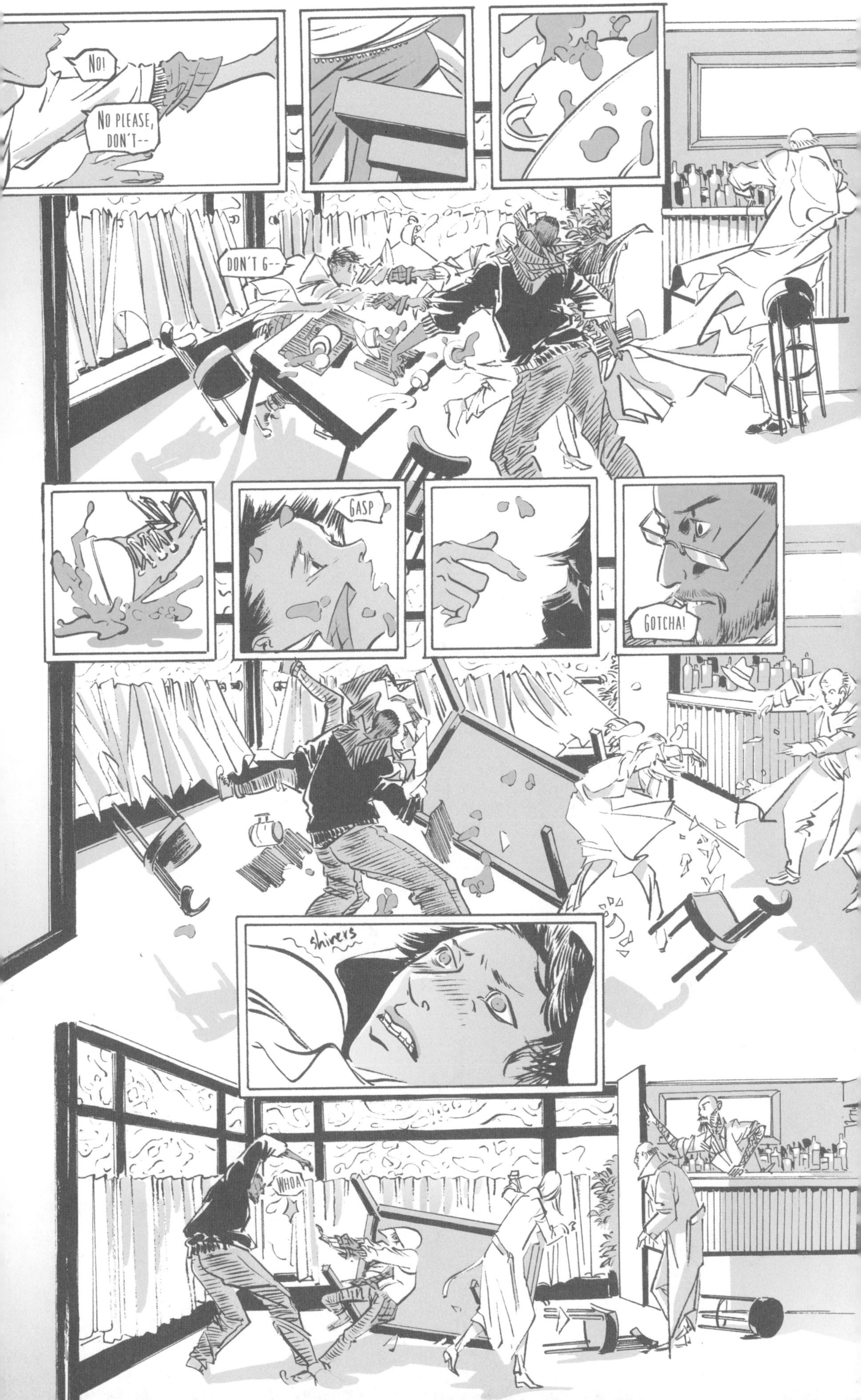
NO!
NO PLEASE, DON'T--
DON'T G--
GASP
GOTCHA!
shivers
WHOA

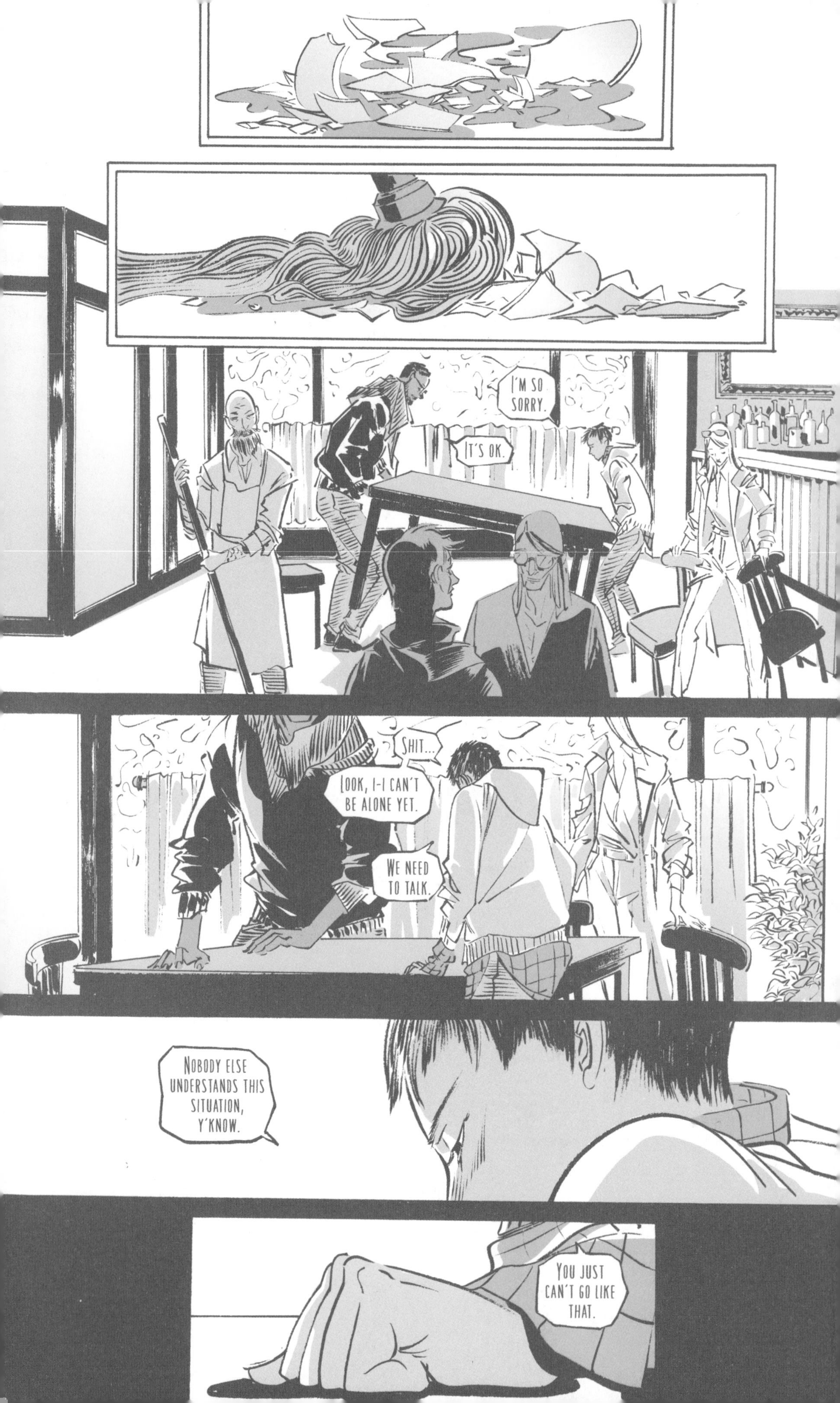
I'M SO SORRY.
IT'S OK.
SHIT...
LOOK, I-I CAN'T BE ALONE YET.
WE NEED TO TALK.
NOBODY ELSE UNDERSTANDS THIS SITUATION, Y'KNOW.
YOU JUST CAN'T GO LIKE THAT.

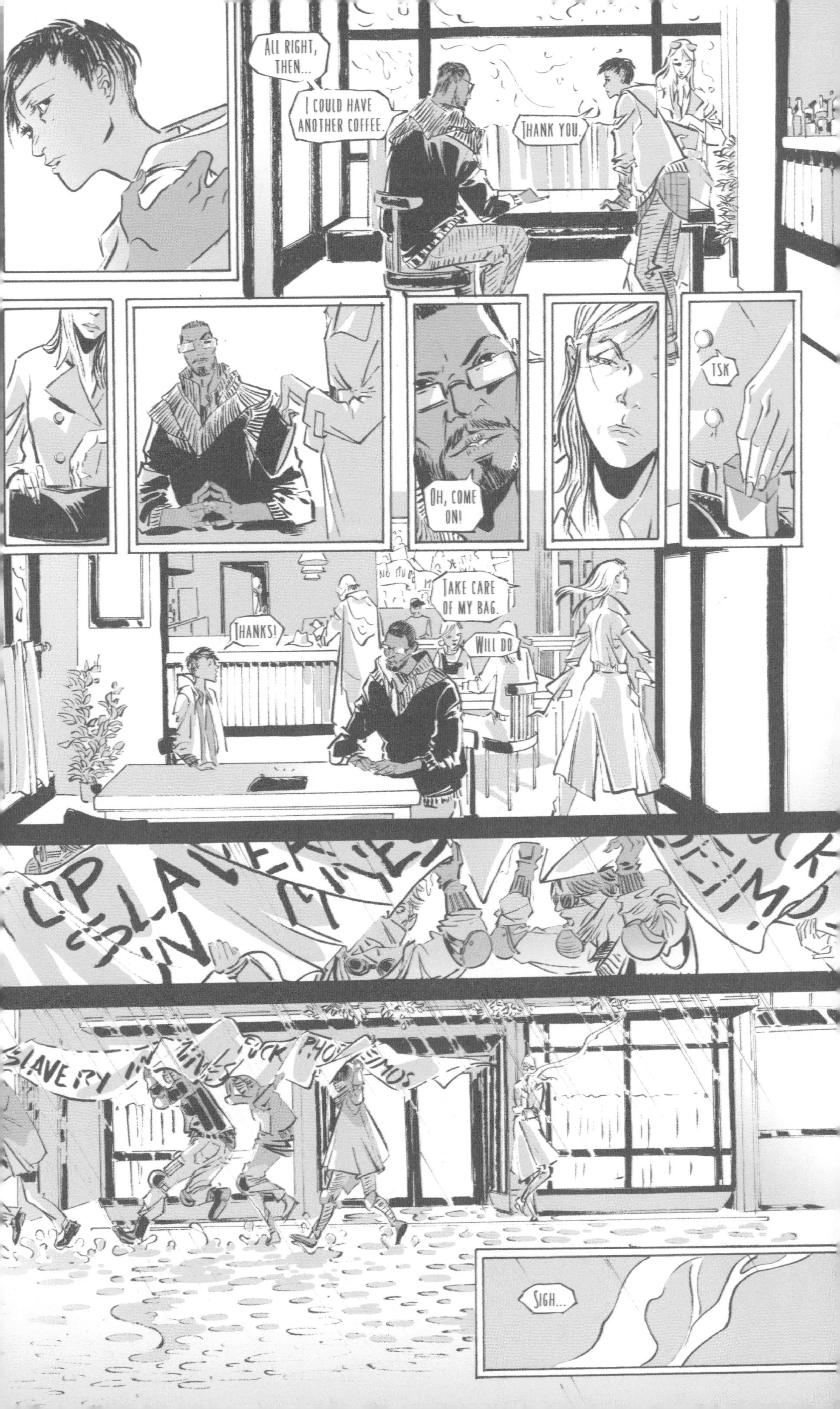

All right, then...
I could have another coffee.
Thank you.
Oh, come on!
TSK
Take care of my bag.
Thanks!
Will do
Sigh...

Chapter 2: The Body Changers

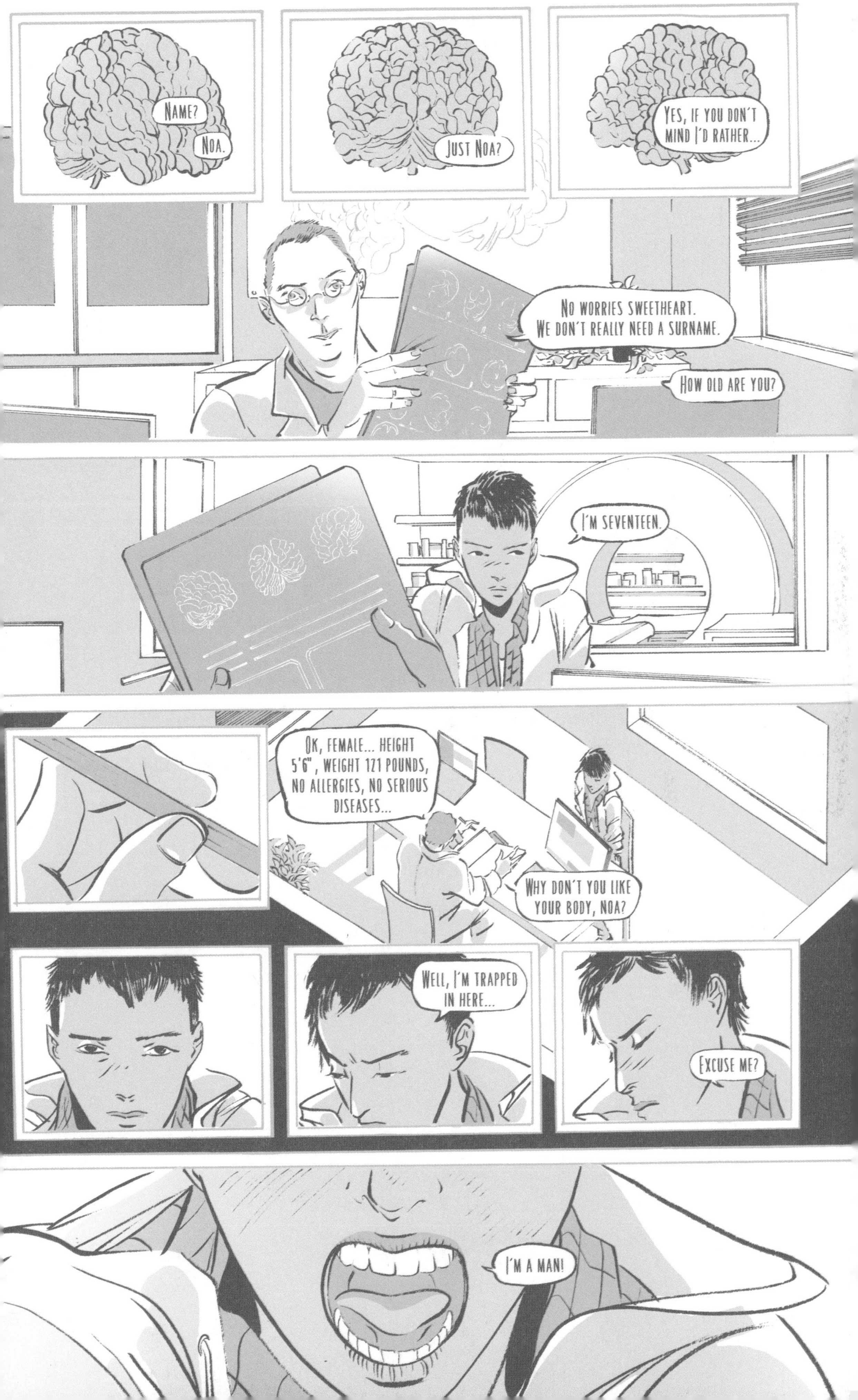
NAME?
NOA.
JUST NOA?
YES, IF YOU DON'T MIND I'D RATHER...
NO WORRIES SWEETHEART. WE DON'T REALLY NEED A SURNAME.
HOW OLD ARE YOU?
I'M SEVENTEEN.
OK, FEMALE... HEIGHT 5'6", WEIGHT 121 POUNDS, NO ALLERGIES, NO SERIOUS DISEASES...
WHY DON'T YOU LIKE YOUR BODY, NOA?
WELL, I'M TRAPPED IN HERE...
EXCUSE ME?
I'M A MAN!

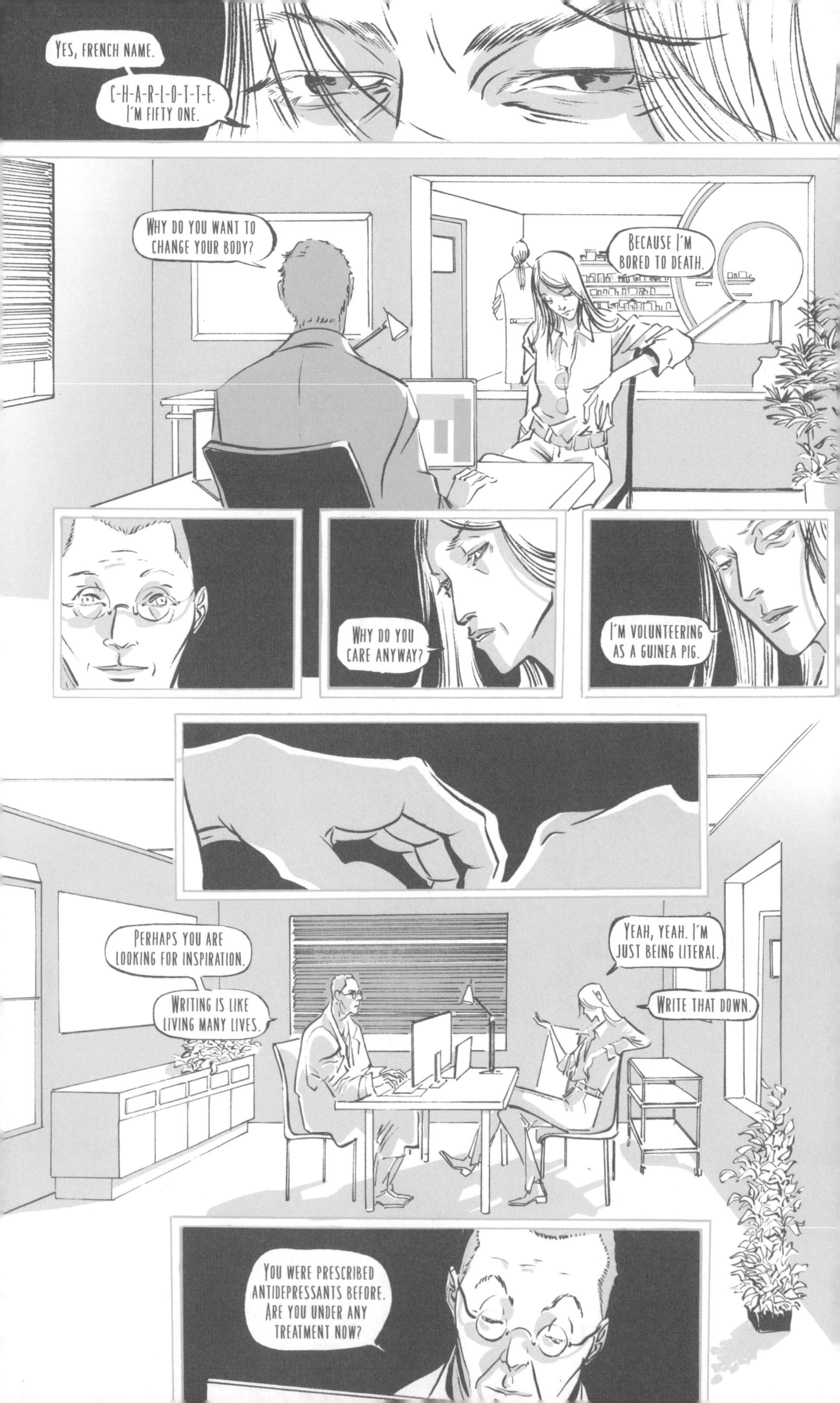
YES, FRENCH NAME.
C-H-A-R-L-O-T-T-E. I'M FIFTY ONE.
WHY DO YOU WANT TO CHANGE YOUR BODY?
BECAUSE I'M BORED TO DEATH.
WHY DO YOU CARE ANYWAY?
I'M VOLUNTEERING AS A GUINEA PIG.
PERHAPS YOU ARE LOOKING FOR INSPIRATION.
WRITING IS LIKE LIVING MANY LIVES.
YEAH, YEAH. I'M JUST BEING LITERAL.
WRITE THAT DOWN.
YOU WERE PRESCRIBED ANTIDEPRESSANTS BEFORE. ARE YOU UNDER ANY TREATMENT NOW?

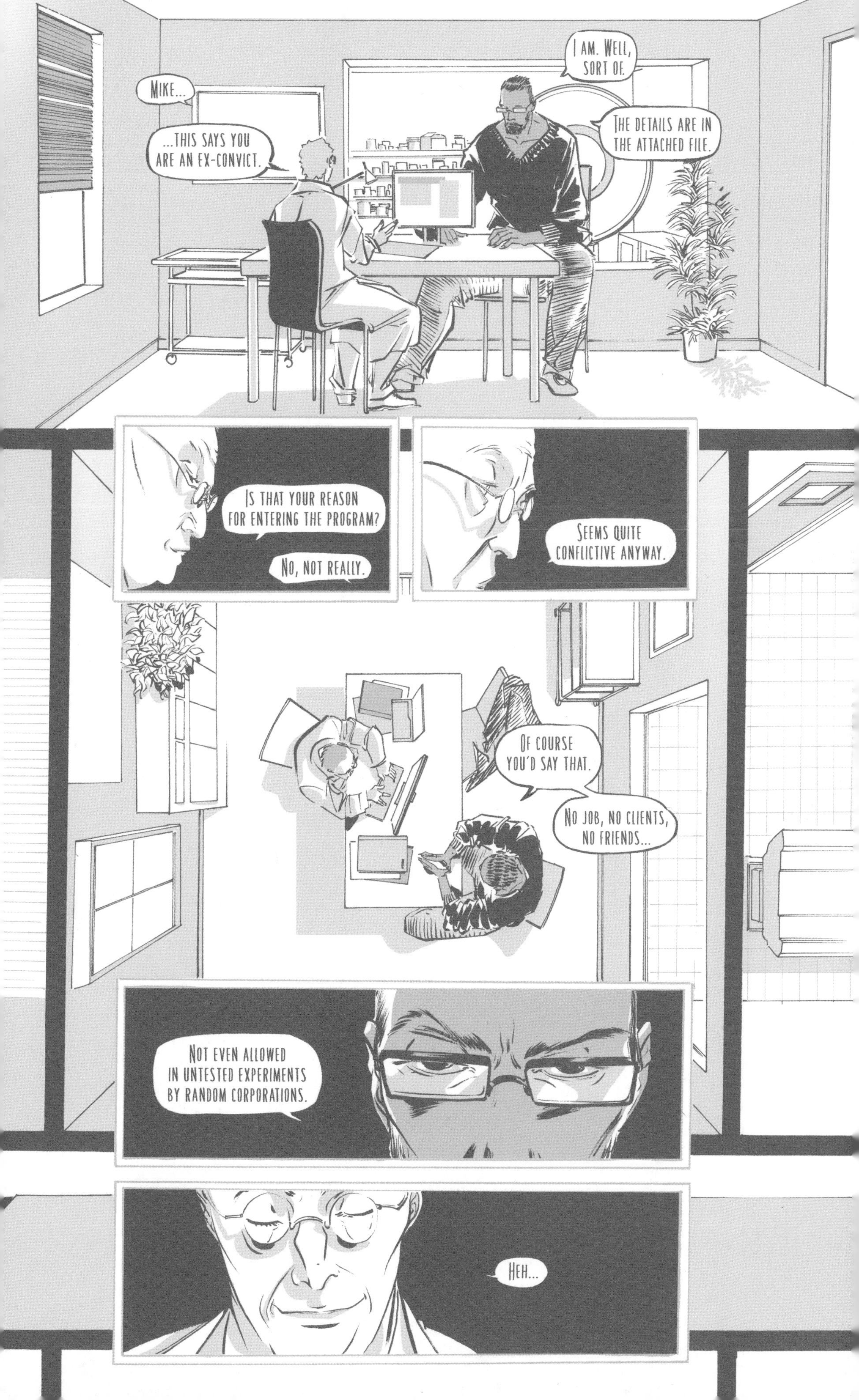
MIKE...
...THIS SAYS YOU ARE AN EX-CONVICT.
I AM. WELL, SORT OF.
THE DETAILS ARE IN THE ATTACHED FILE.
IS THAT YOUR REASON FOR ENTERING THE PROGRAM?
NO, NOT REALLY.
SEEMS QUITE CONFLICTIVE ANYWAY.
OF COURSE YOU'D SAY THAT.
NO JOB, NO CLIENTS, NO FRIENDS...
NOT EVEN ALLOWED IN UNTESTED EXPERIMENTS BY RANDOM CORPORATIONS.
HEH...

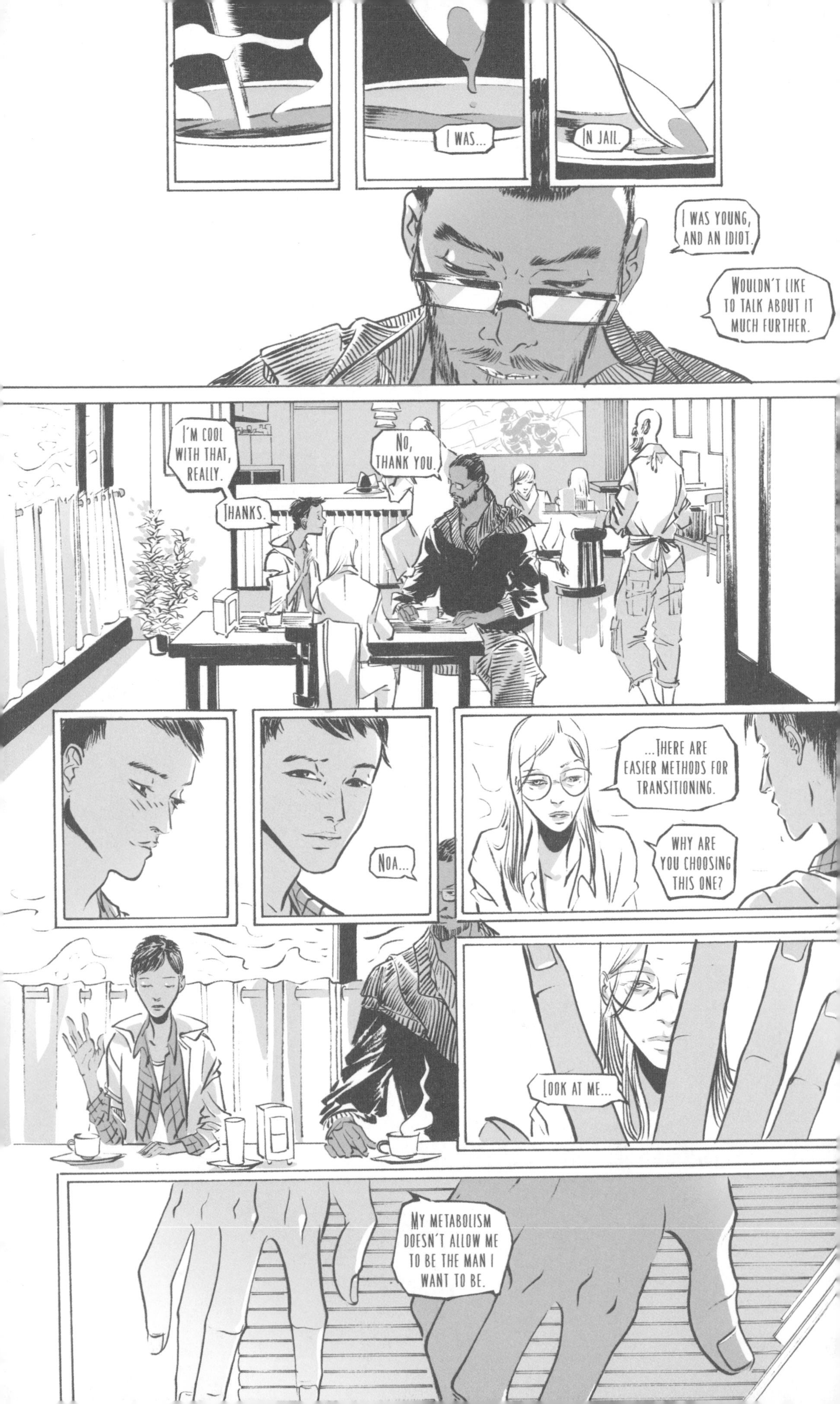
I WAS...
IN JAIL.
I WAS YOUNG, AND AN IDIOT.
WOULDN'T LIKE TO TALK ABOUT IT MUCH FURTHER.
I'M COOL WITH THAT, REALLY.
THANKS.
NO, THANK YOU.
NOA...
...THERE ARE EASIER METHODS FOR TRANSITIONING.
WHY ARE YOU CHOOSING THIS ONE?
LOOK AT ME...
MY METABOLISM DOESN'T ALLOW ME TO BE THE MAN I WANT TO BE.

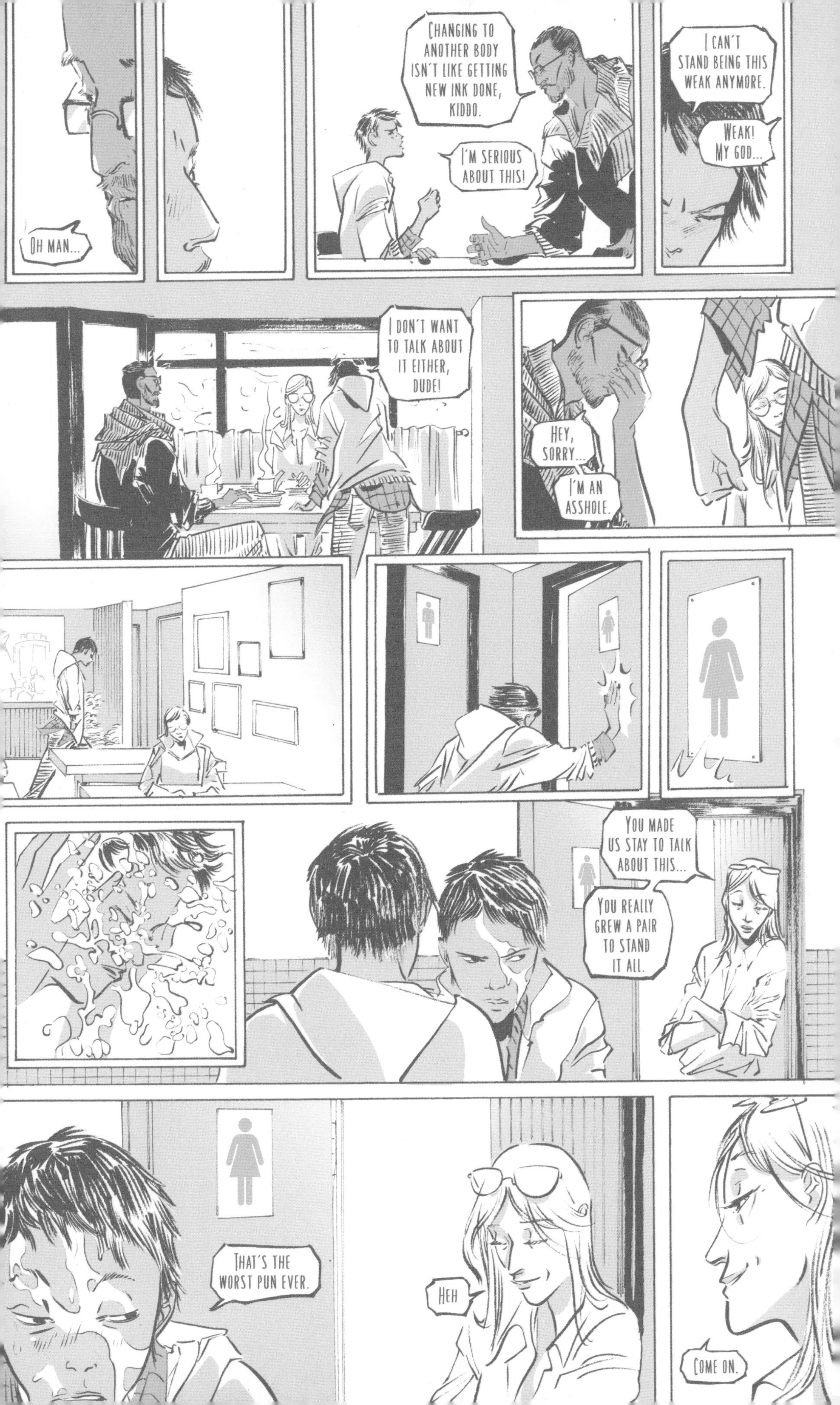
OH MAN...
CHANGING TO ANOTHER BODY ISN'T LIKE GETTING NEW INK DONE, KIDDO.
I'M SERIOUS ABOUT THIS!
I CAN'T STAND BEING THIS WEAK ANYMORE.
WEAK! MY GOD...
I DON'T WANT TO TALK ABOUT IT EITHER, DUDE!
HEY, SORRY...
I'M AN ASSHOLE.
YOU MADE US STAY TO TALK ABOUT THIS...
YOU REALLY GREW A PAIR TO STAND IT ALL.
THAT'S THE WORST PUN EVER.
HEH
COME ON.

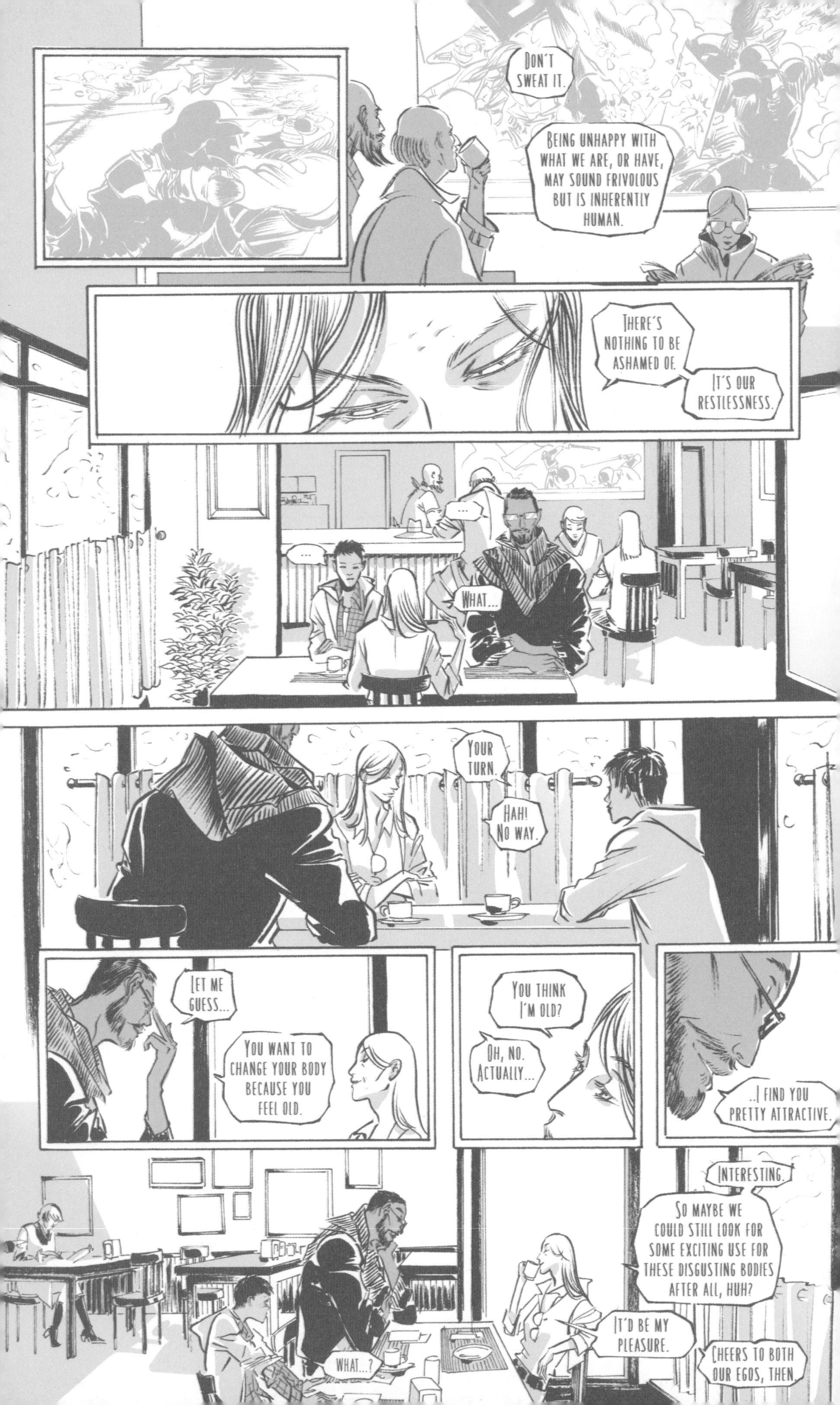

Don't sweat it.
Being unhappy with what we are, or have, may sound frivolous but is inherently human.
There's nothing to be ashamed of.
It's our restlessness.
...
...
What...
Your turn.
Hah! No way.
Let me guess...
You want to change your body because you feel old.
You think I'm old?
Oh, no. Actually...
..I find you pretty attractive.
Interesting.
So maybe we could still look for some exciting use for these disgusting bodies after all, huh?
It'd be my pleasure.
What...?
Cheers to both our egos, then.

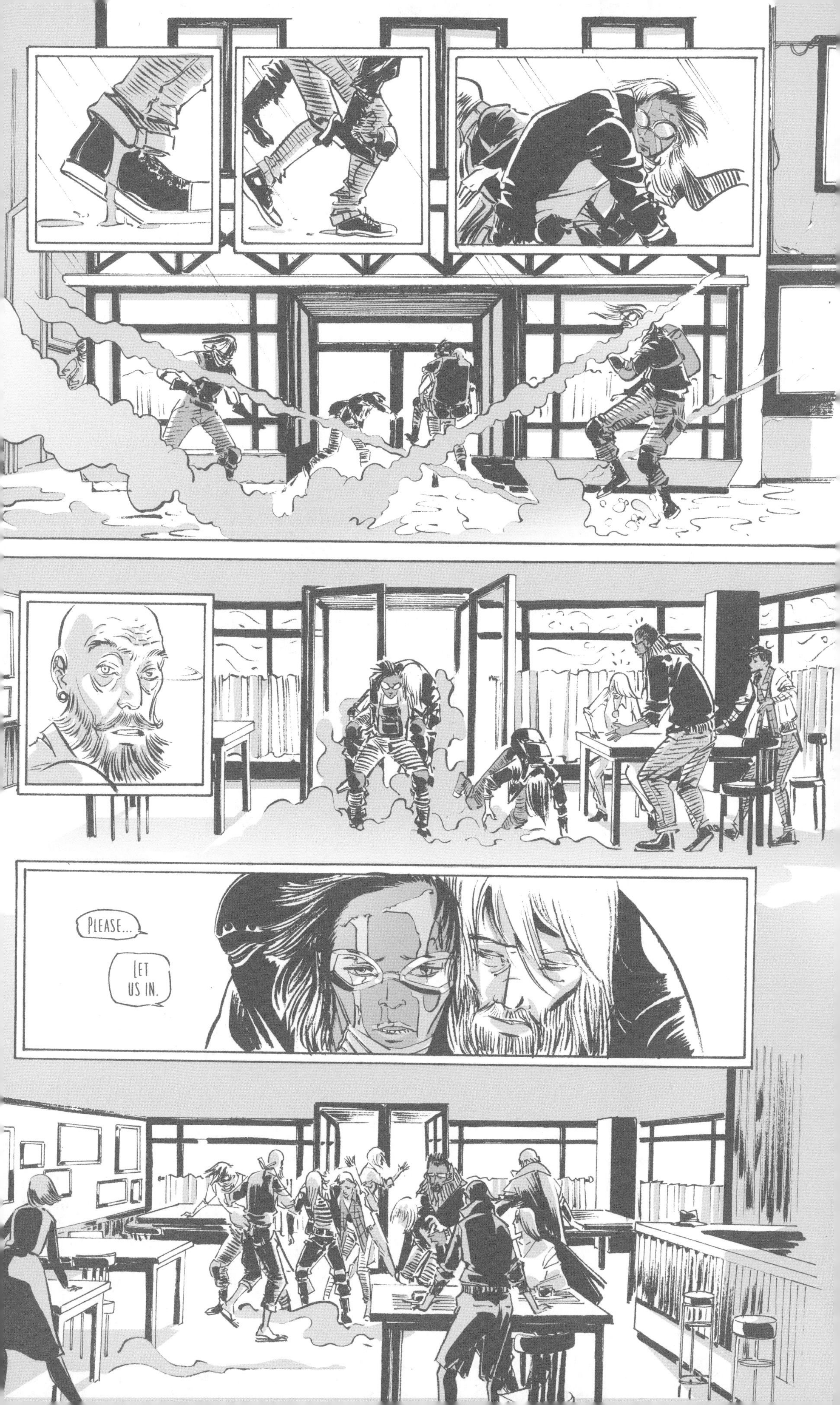
PLEASE...
LET US IN.

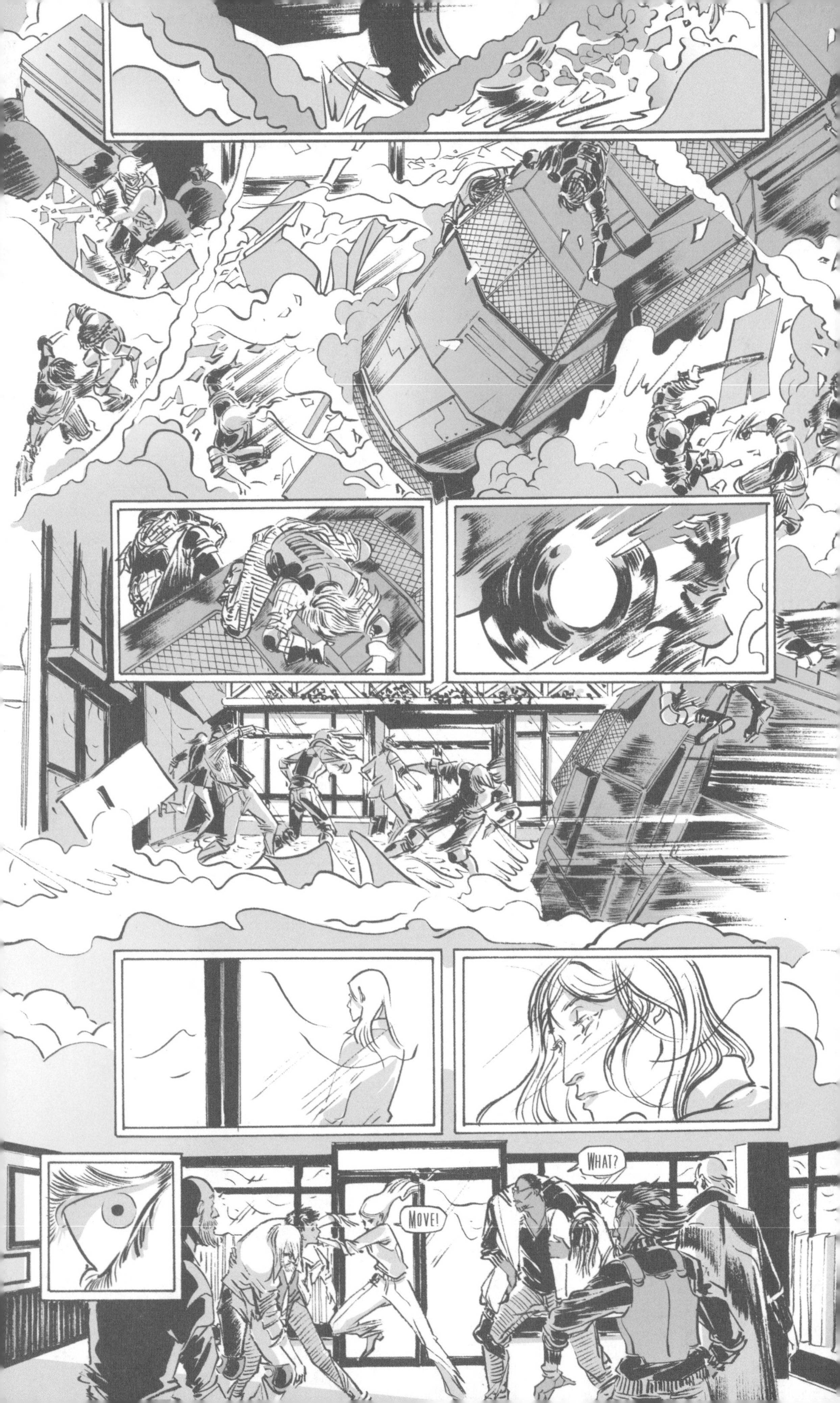
Move!
What?

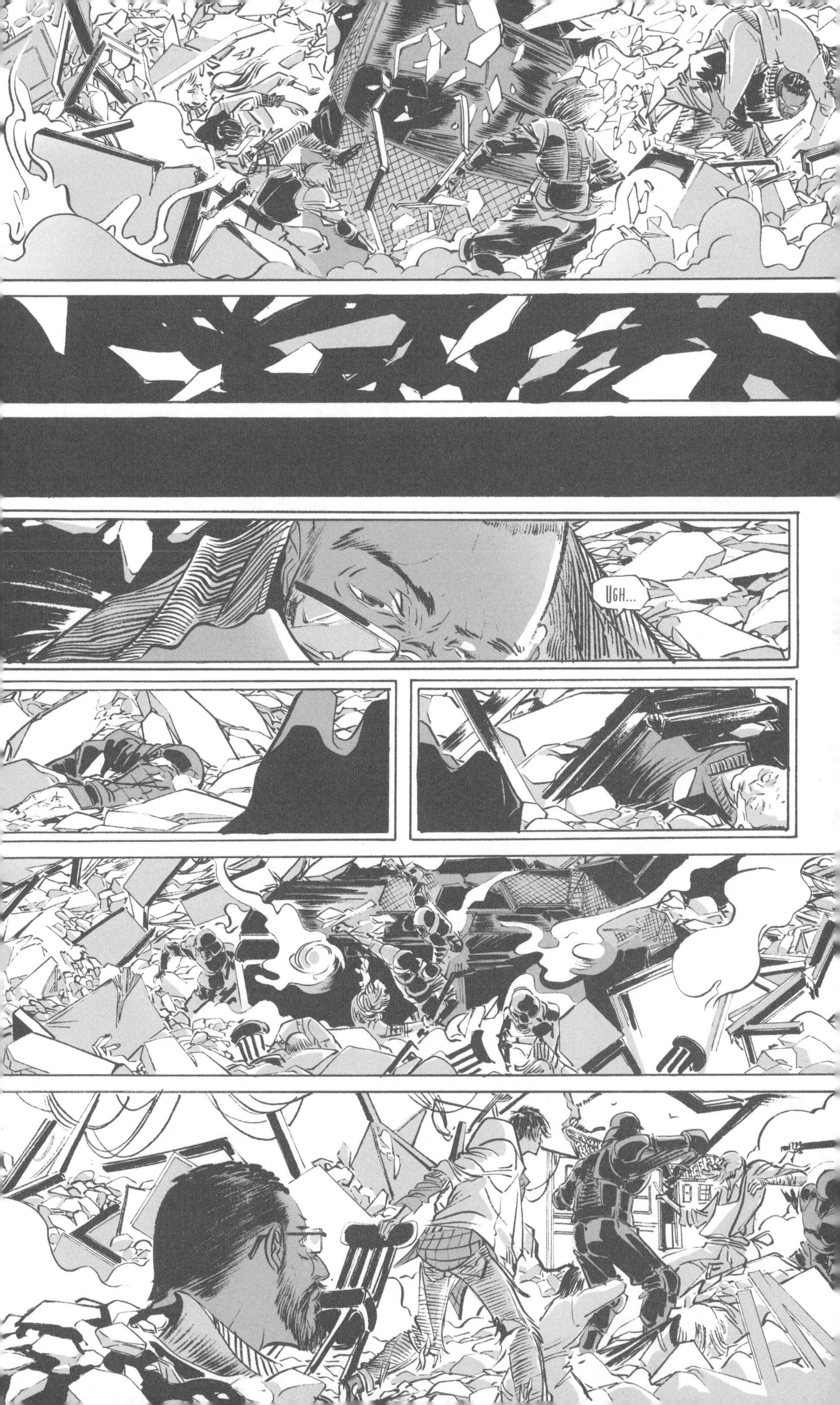
UGH...

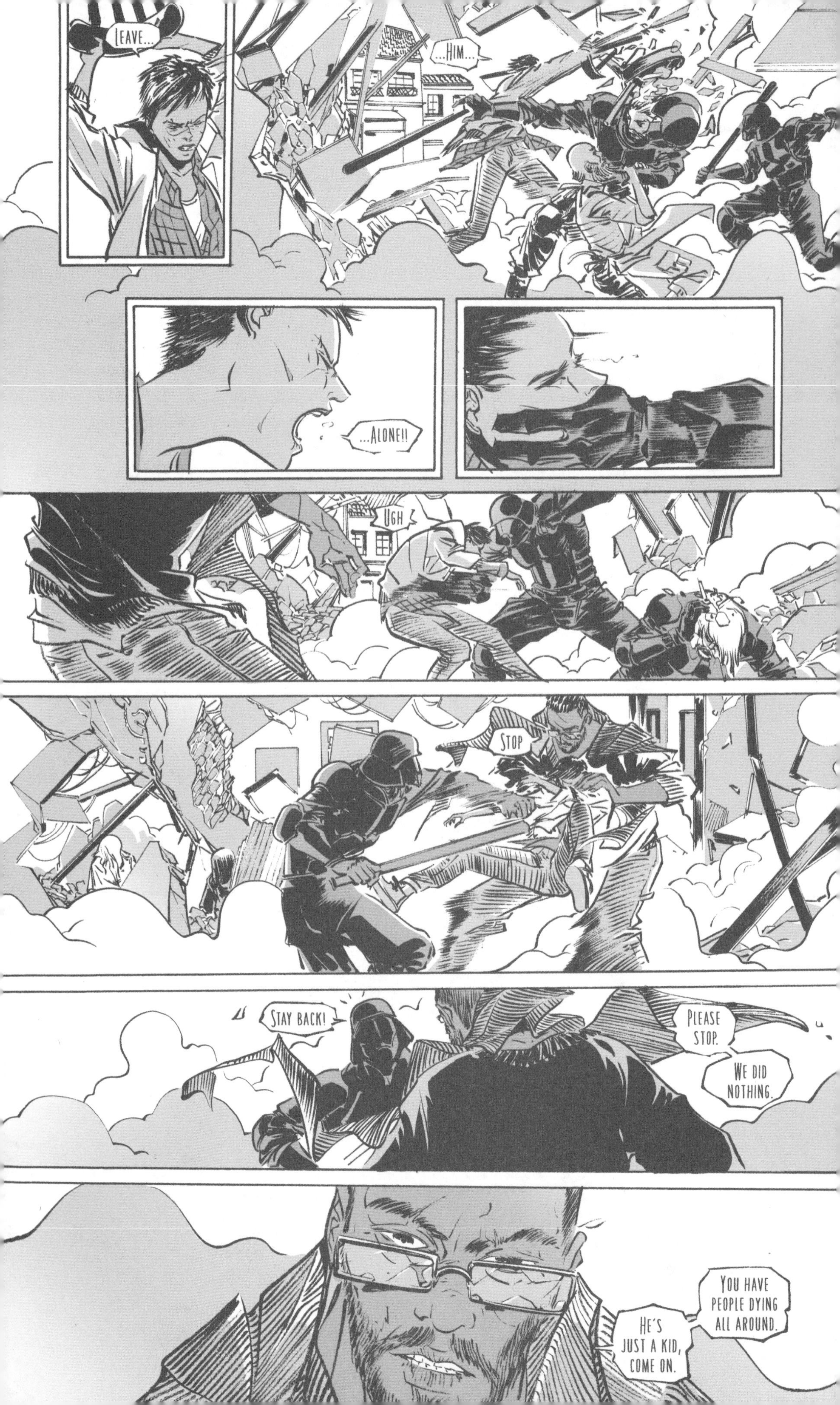
LEAVE...
...HIM...
...ALONE!!
UGH
STOP
STAY BACK!
PLEASE STOP.
WE DID NOTHING.
YOU HAVE PEOPLE DYING ALL AROUND.
HE'S JUST A KID, COME ON.

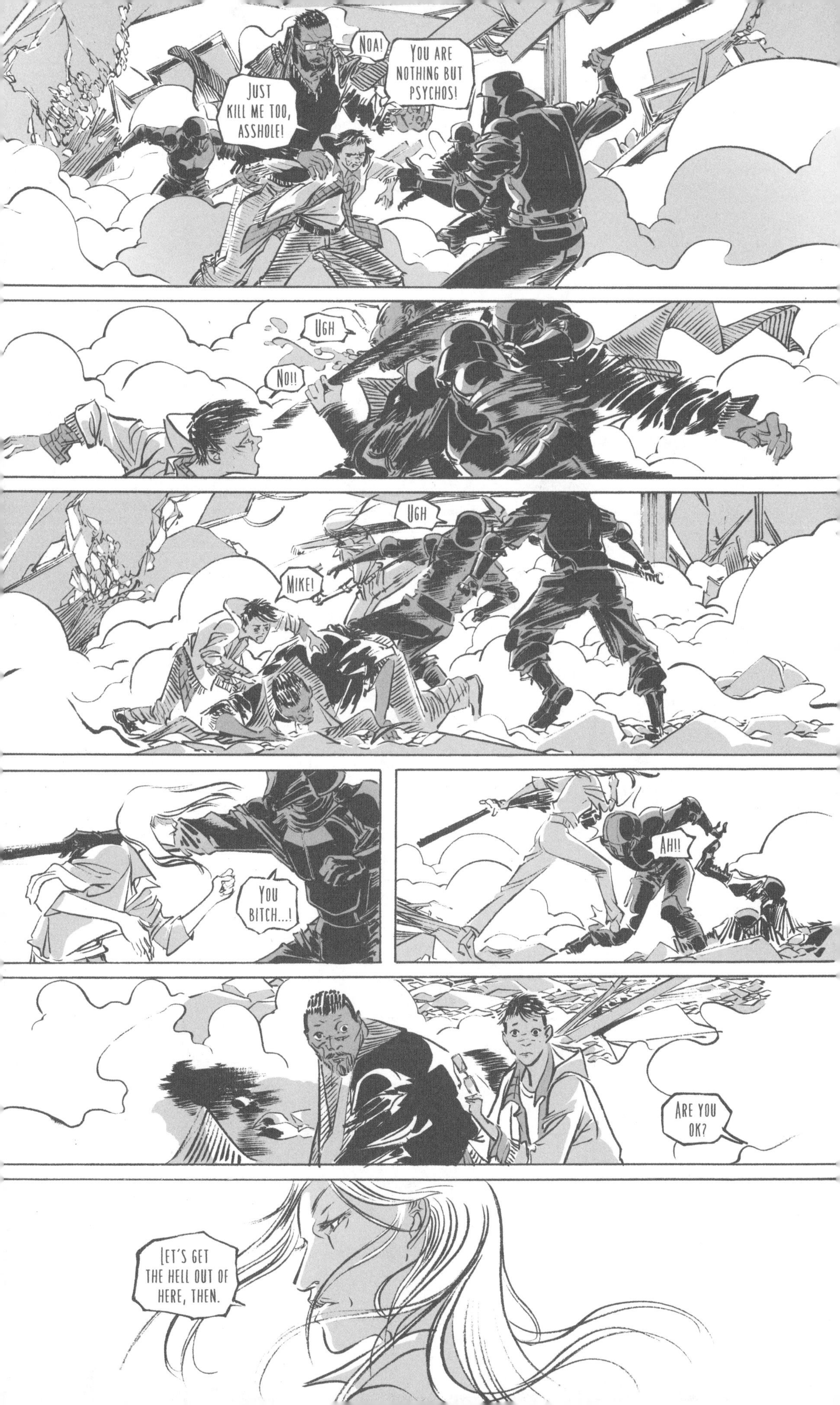
Noa!
You are nothing but psychos!
Just kill me too, asshole!
Ugh
No!!
Ugh
Mike!
You bitch...!
Ah!!
Are you OK?
Let's get the hell out of here, then.

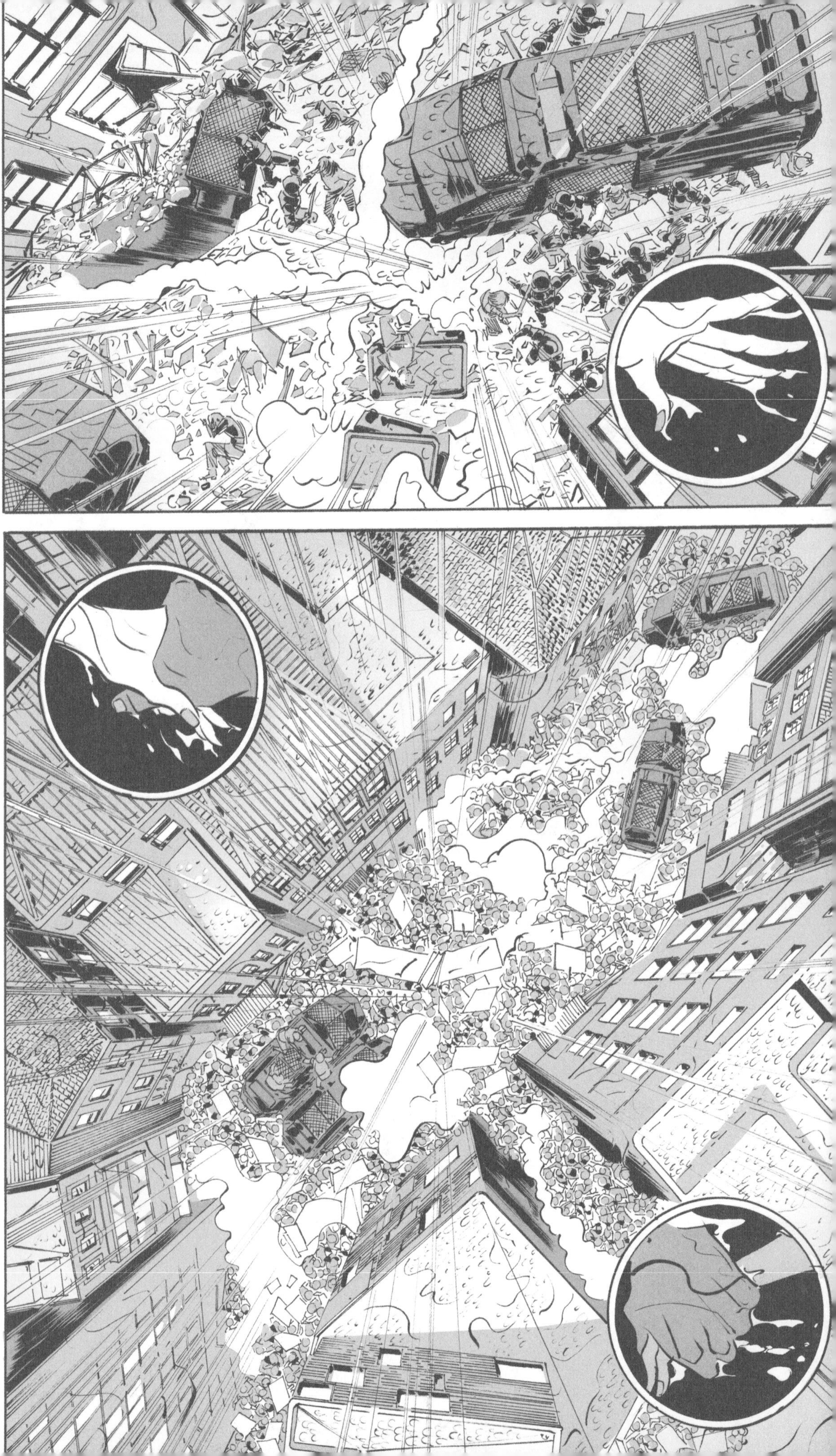

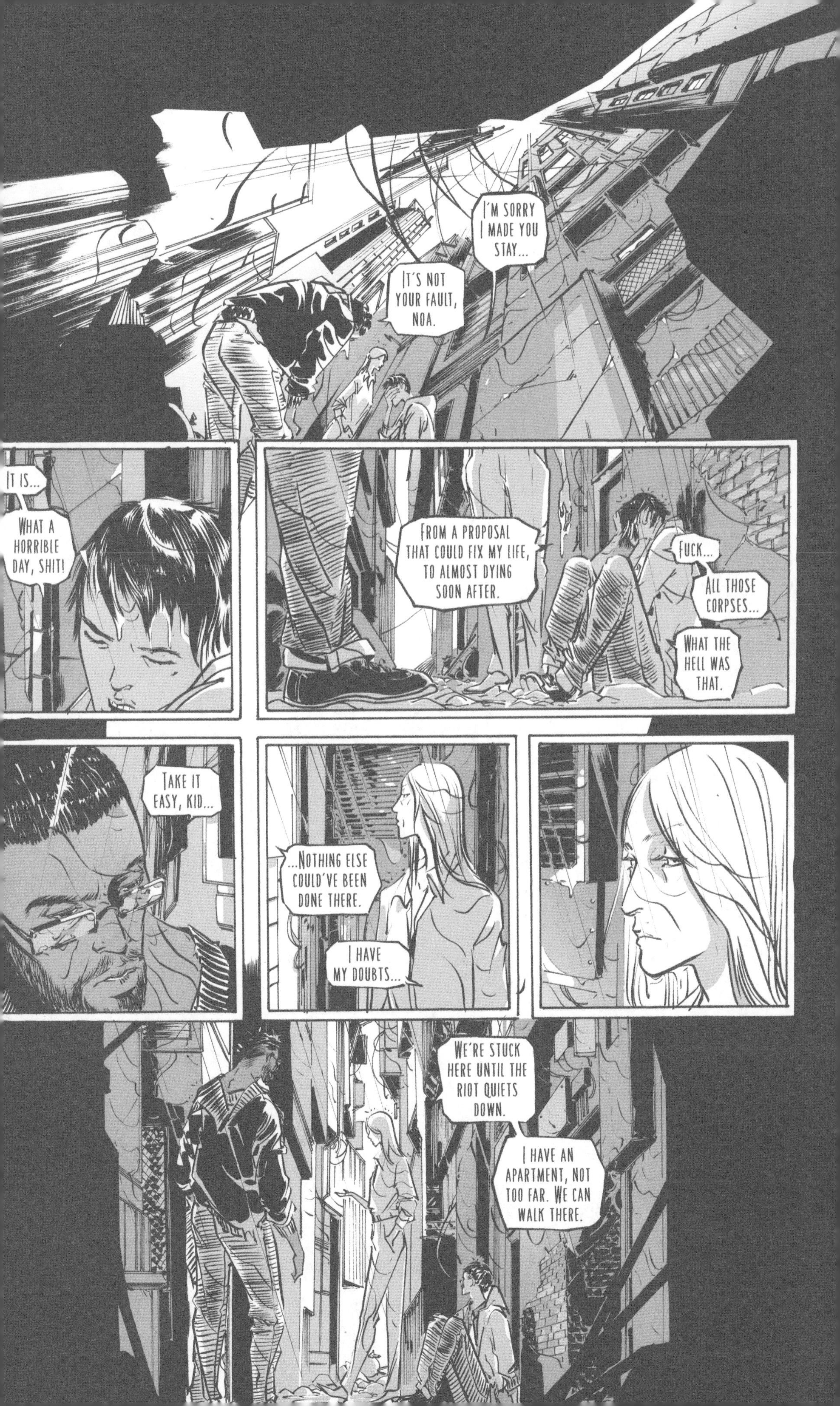
I'M SORRY I MADE YOU STAY...
IT'S NOT YOUR FAULT, NOA.
IT IS...
WHAT A HORRIBLE DAY, SHIT!
FROM A PROPOSAL THAT COULD FIX MY LIFE, TO ALMOST DYING SOON AFTER.
FUCK...
ALL THOSE CORPSES...
WHAT THE HELL WAS THAT.
TAKE IT EASY, KID...
...NOTHING ELSE COULD'VE BEEN DONE THERE.
I HAVE MY DOUBTS...
WE'RE STUCK HERE UNTIL THE RIOT QUIETS DOWN.
I HAVE AN APARTMENT, NOT TOO FAR. WE CAN WALK THERE.

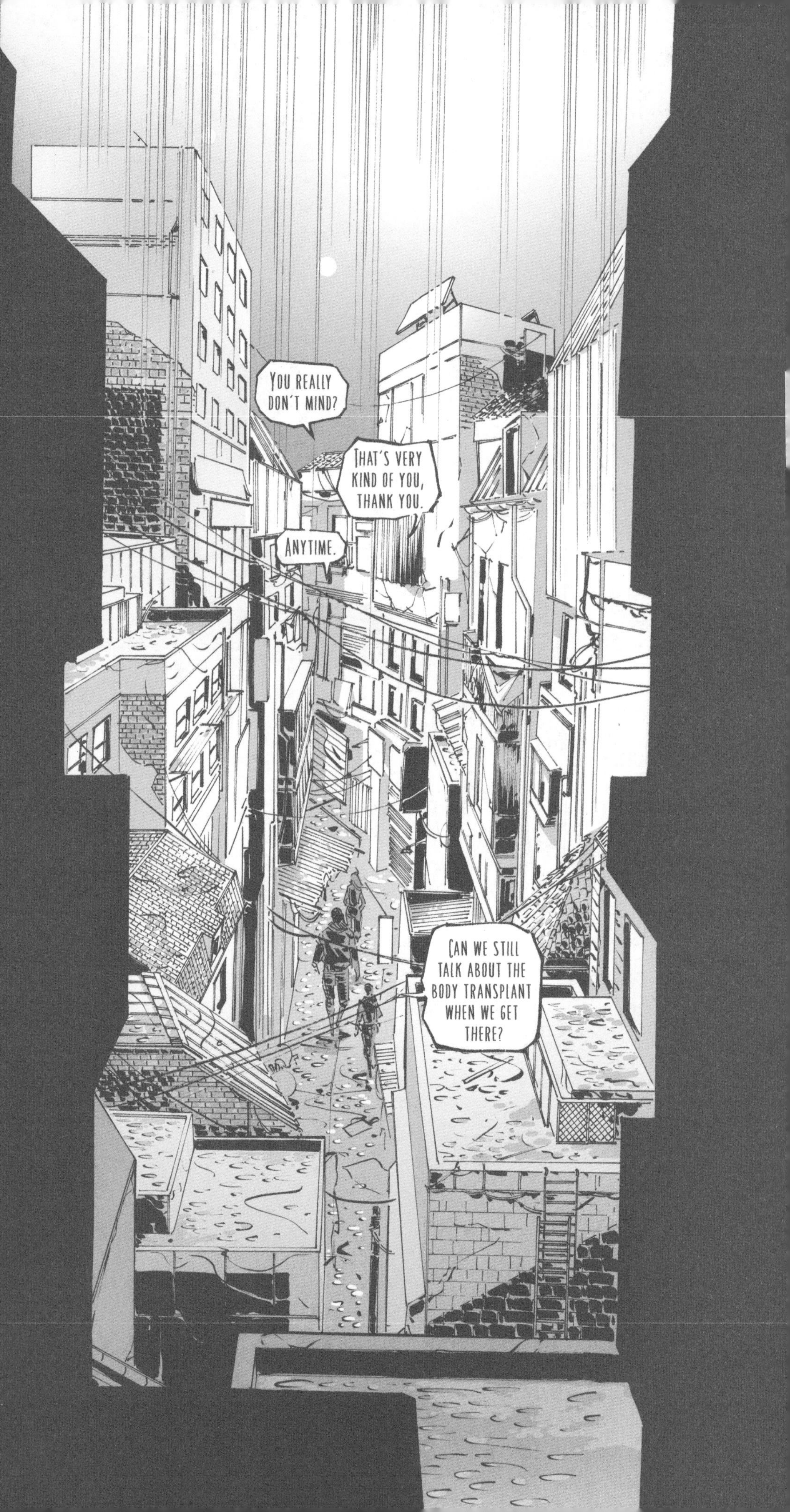
YOU REALLY DON'T MIND?
THAT'S VERY KIND OF YOU, THANK YOU.
ANYTIME.
CAN WE STILL TALK ABOUT THE BODY TRANSPLANT WHEN WE GET THERE?

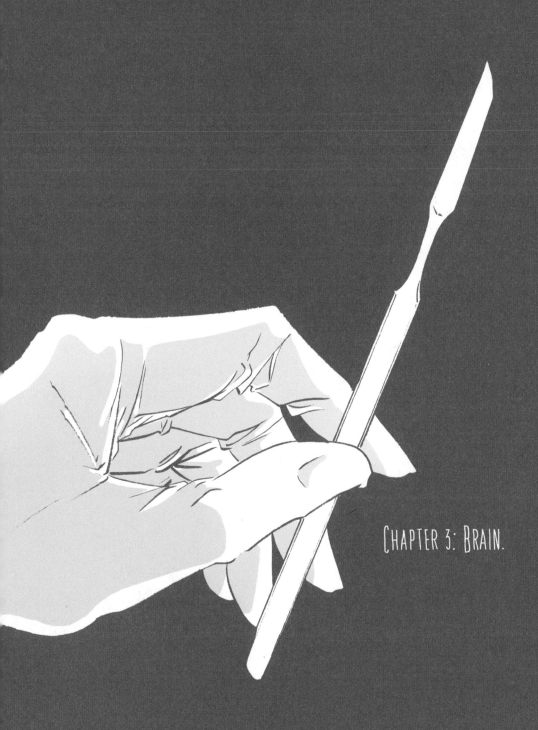

CHAPTER 3: BRAIN.

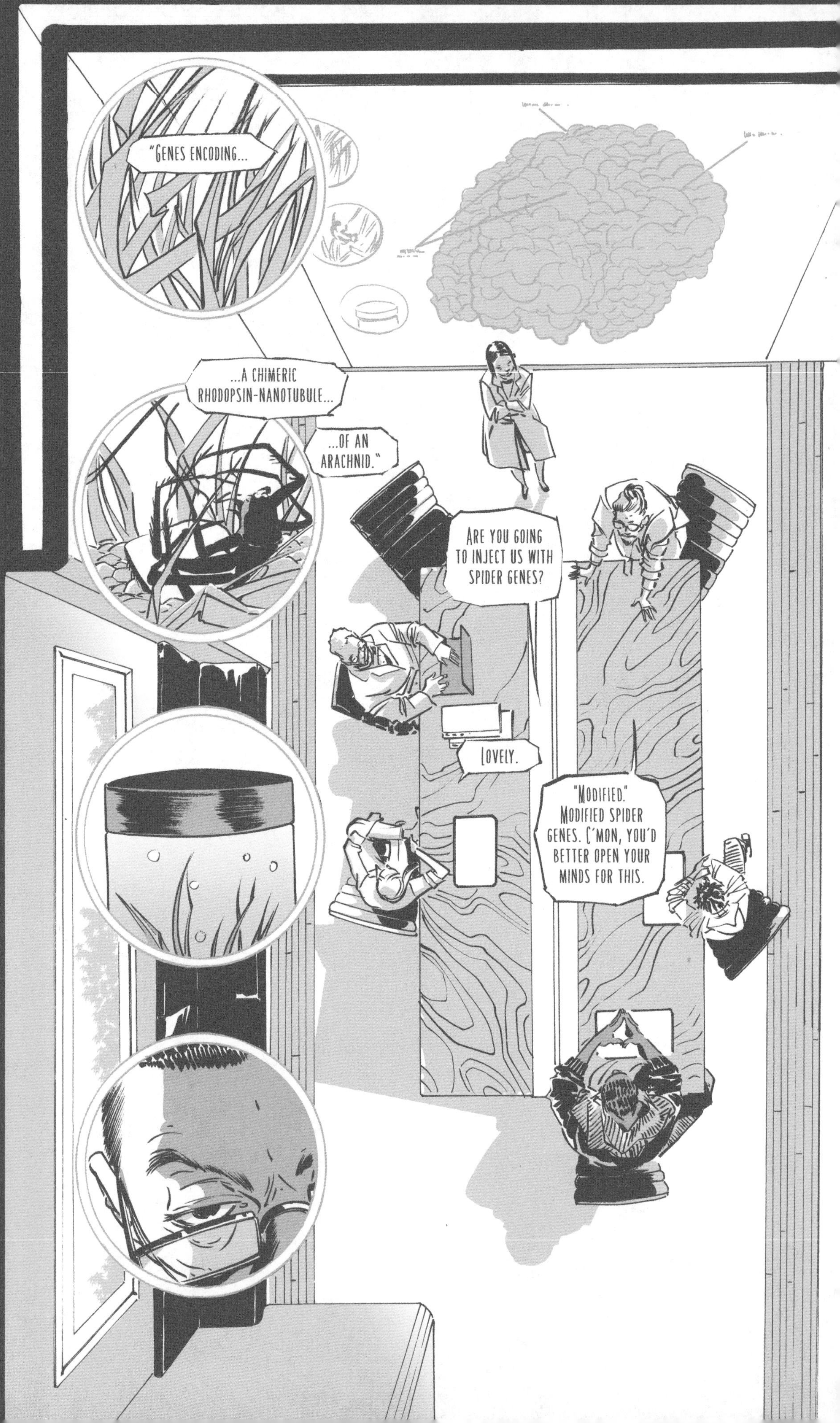
"Genes encoding...
...a chimeric rhodopsin-nanotubule...
...of an arachnid."
Are you going to inject us with spider genes?
Lovely.
"Modified." Modified spider genes. C'mon, you'd better open your minds for this.

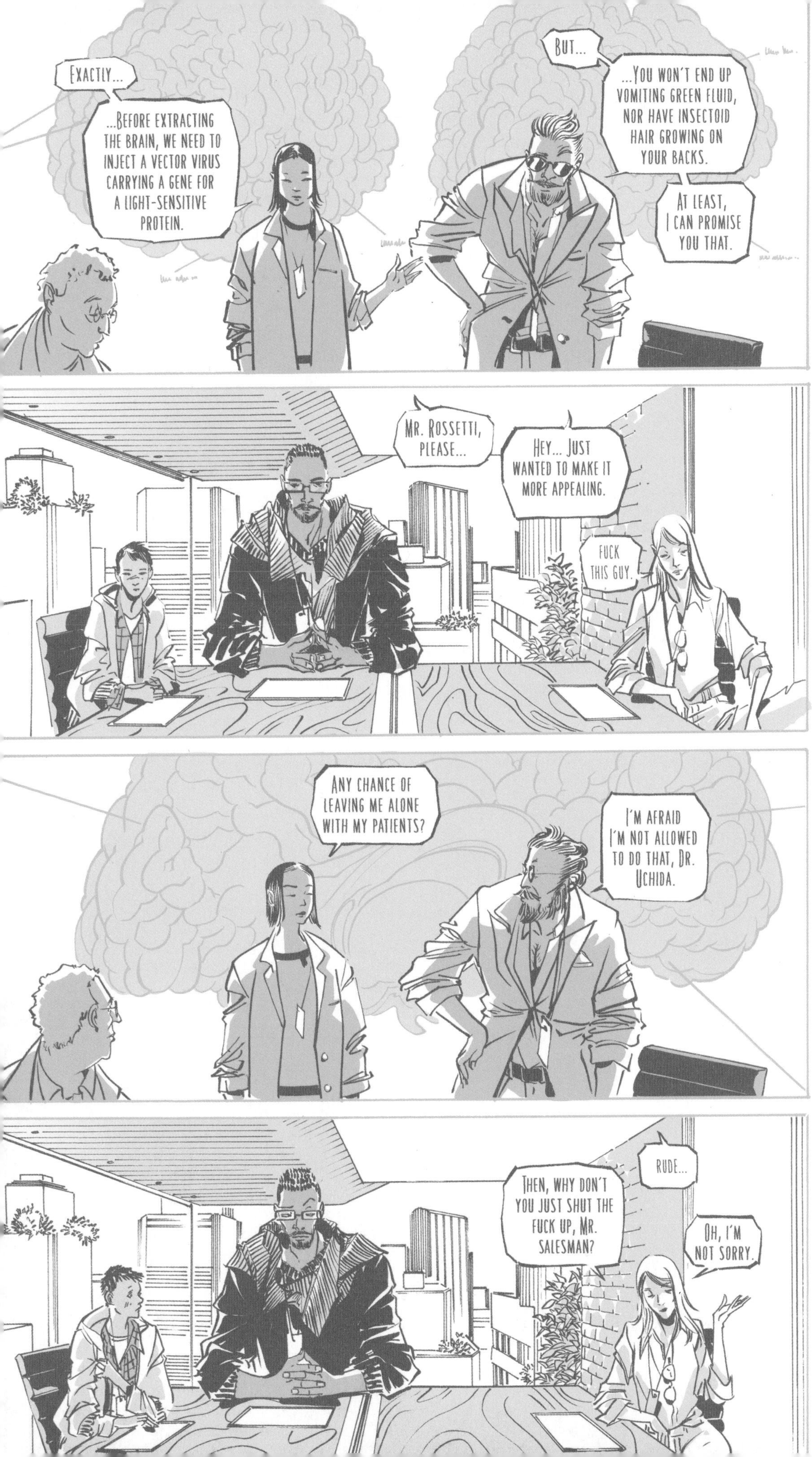

Exactly...
...Before extracting the brain, we need to inject a vector virus carrying a gene for a light-sensitive protein.
But...
...You won't end up vomiting green fluid, nor have insectoid hair growing on your backs.
At least, I can promise you that.
Mr. Rossetti, please...
Hey... Just wanted to make it more appealing.
Fuck this guy.
Any chance of leaving me alone with my patients?
I'm afraid I'm not allowed to do that, Dr. Uchida.
Then, why don't you just shut the fuck up, Mr. Salesman?
Rude...
Oh, I'm not sorry.

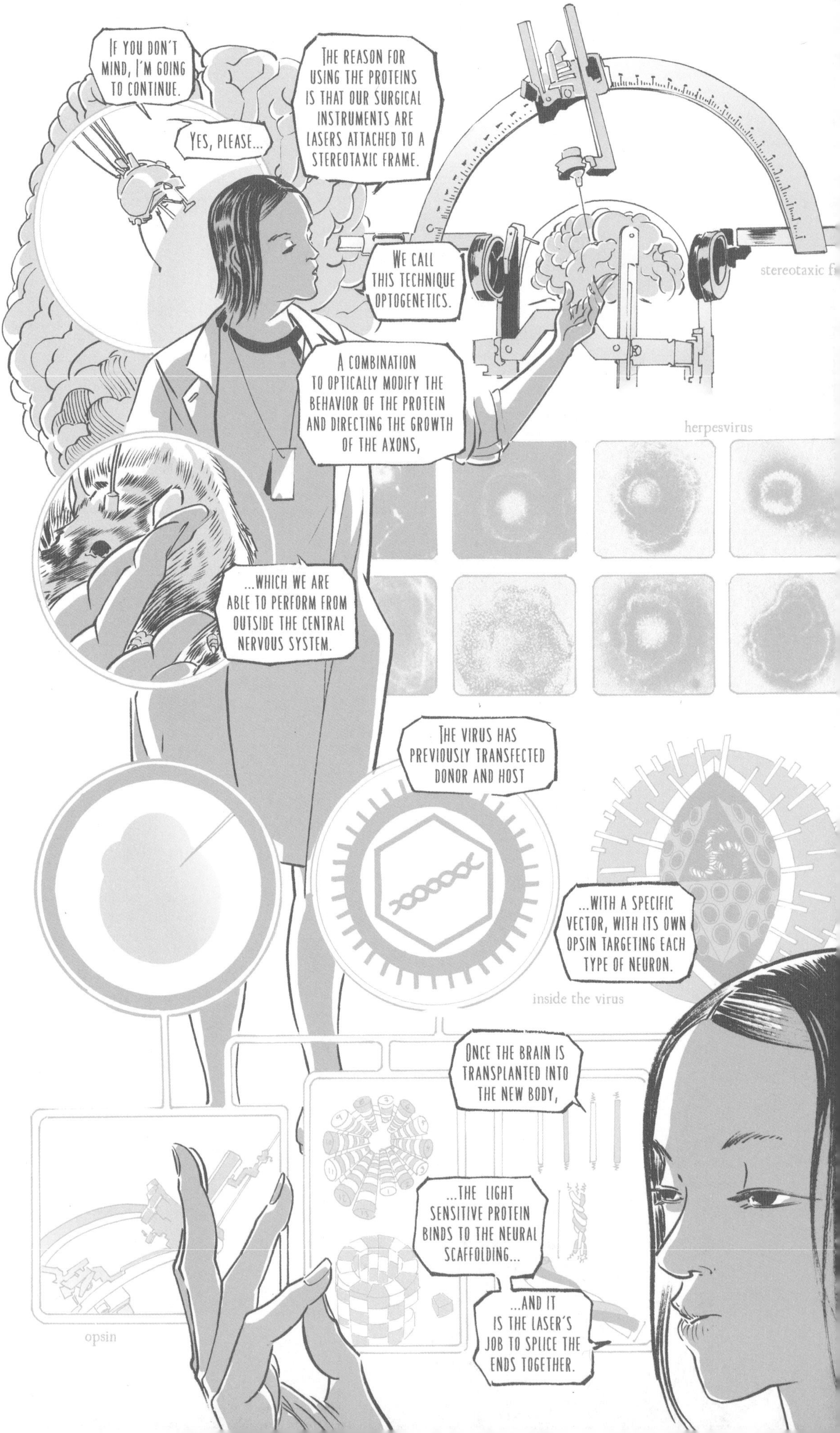

IF YOU DON'T MIND, I'M GOING TO CONTINUE.
YES, PLEASE...
THE REASON FOR USING THE PROTEINS IS THAT OUR SURGICAL INSTRUMENTS ARE LASERS ATTACHED TO A STEREOTAXIC FRAME.
WE CALL THIS TECHNIQUE OPTOGENETICS.
A COMBINATION TO OPTICALLY MODIFY THE BEHAVIOR OF THE PROTEIN AND DIRECTING THE GROWTH OF THE AXONS,
...WHICH WE ARE ABLE TO PERFORM FROM OUTSIDE THE CENTRAL NERVOUS SYSTEM.
herpesvirus
THE VIRUS HAS PREVIOUSLY TRANSFECTED DONOR AND HOST
...WITH A SPECIFIC VECTOR, WITH ITS OWN OPSIN TARGETING EACH TYPE OF NEURON.
inside the virus
ONCE THE BRAIN IS TRANSPLANTED INTO THE NEW BODY,
...THE LIGHT SENSITIVE PROTEIN BINDS TO THE NEURAL SCAFFOLDING...
...AND IT IS THE LASER'S JOB TO SPLICE THE ENDS TOGETHER.
opsin

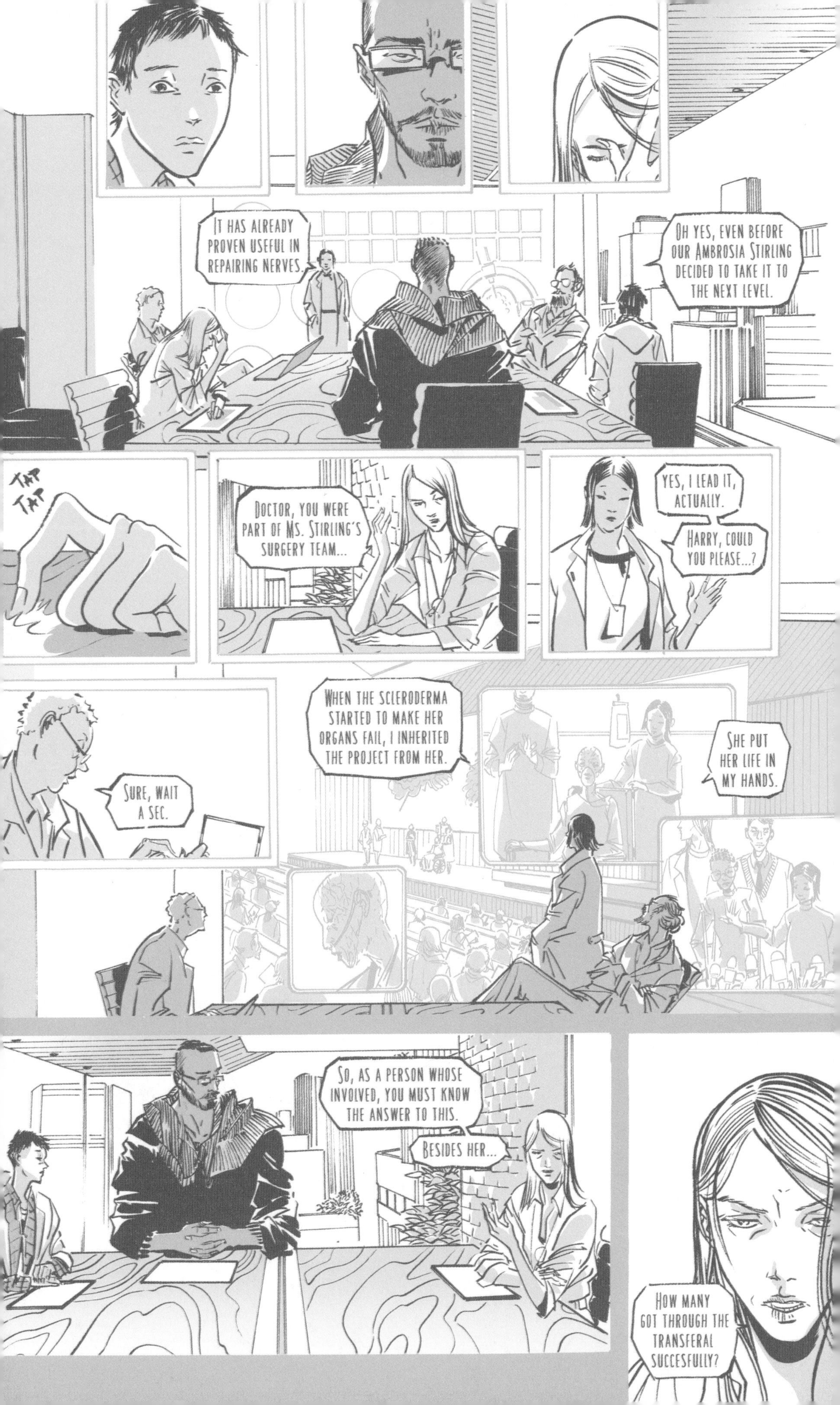
It has already proven useful in repairing nerves.
Oh yes, even before our Ambrosia Stirling decided to take it to the next level.
TAP TAP
Doctor, you were part of Ms. Stirling's surgery team...
Yes, I lead it, actually.
Harry, could you please...?
Sure, wait a sec.
When the scleroderma started to make her organs fail, I inherited the project from her.
She put her life in my hands.
So, as a person whose involved, you must know the answer to this.
Besides her...
How many got through the transferal succesfully?

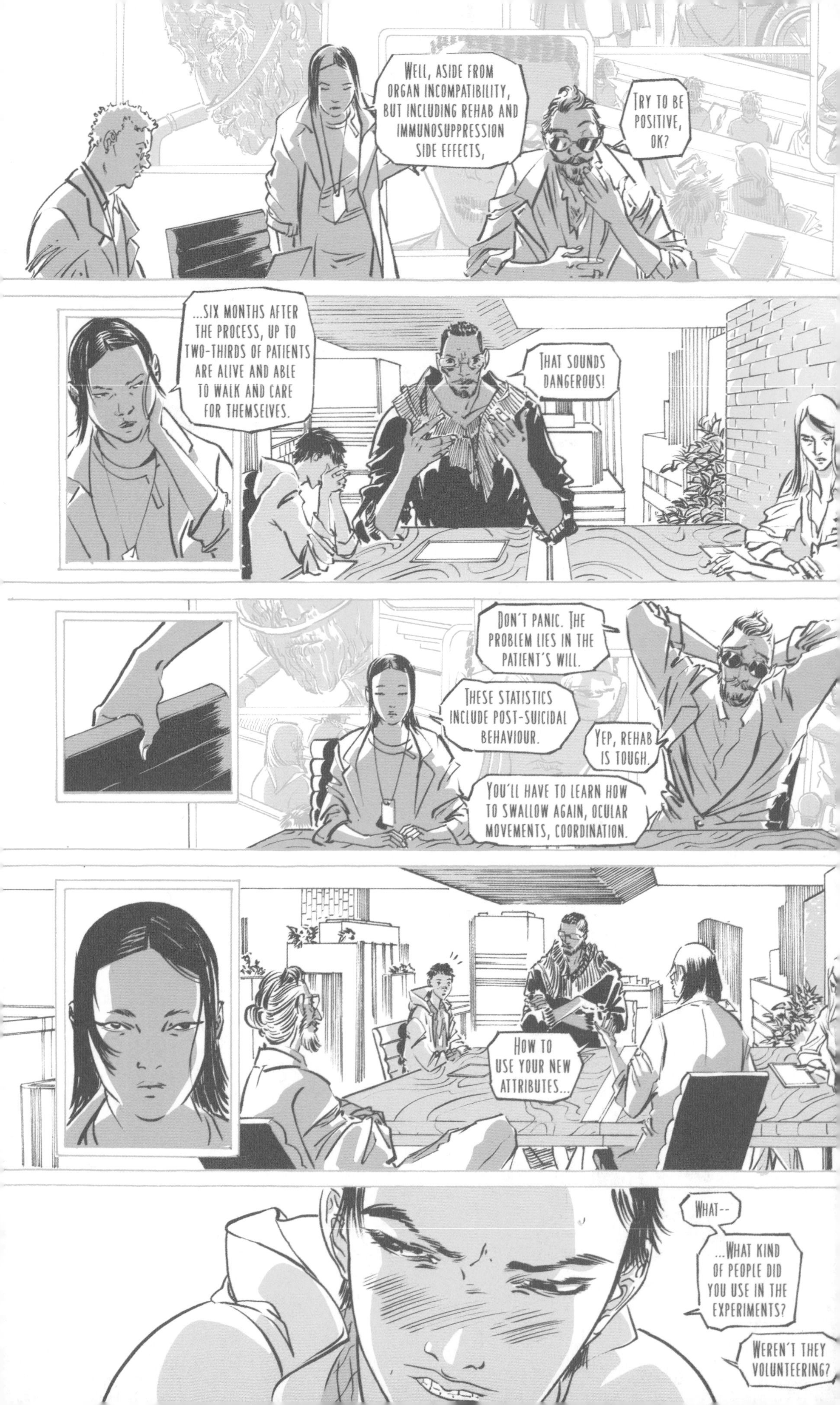
WELL, ASIDE FROM ORGAN INCOMPATIBILITY, BUT INCLUDING REHAB AND IMMUNOSUPPRESSION SIDE EFFECTS,
TRY TO BE POSITIVE, OK?
...SIX MONTHS AFTER THE PROCESS, UP TO TWO-THIRDS OF PATIENTS ARE ALIVE AND ABLE TO WALK AND CARE FOR THEMSELVES.
THAT SOUNDS DANGEROUS!
DON'T PANIC. THE PROBLEM LIES IN THE PATIENT'S WILL.
THESE STATISTICS INCLUDE POST-SUICIDAL BEHAVIOUR.
YEP, REHAB IS TOUGH.
YOU'LL HAVE TO LEARN HOW TO SWALLOW AGAIN, OCULAR MOVEMENTS, COORDINATION.
HOW TO USE YOUR NEW ATTRIBUTES...
WHAT--
...WHAT KIND OF PEOPLE DID YOU USE IN THE EXPERIMENTS?
WEREN'T THEY VOLUNTEERING?

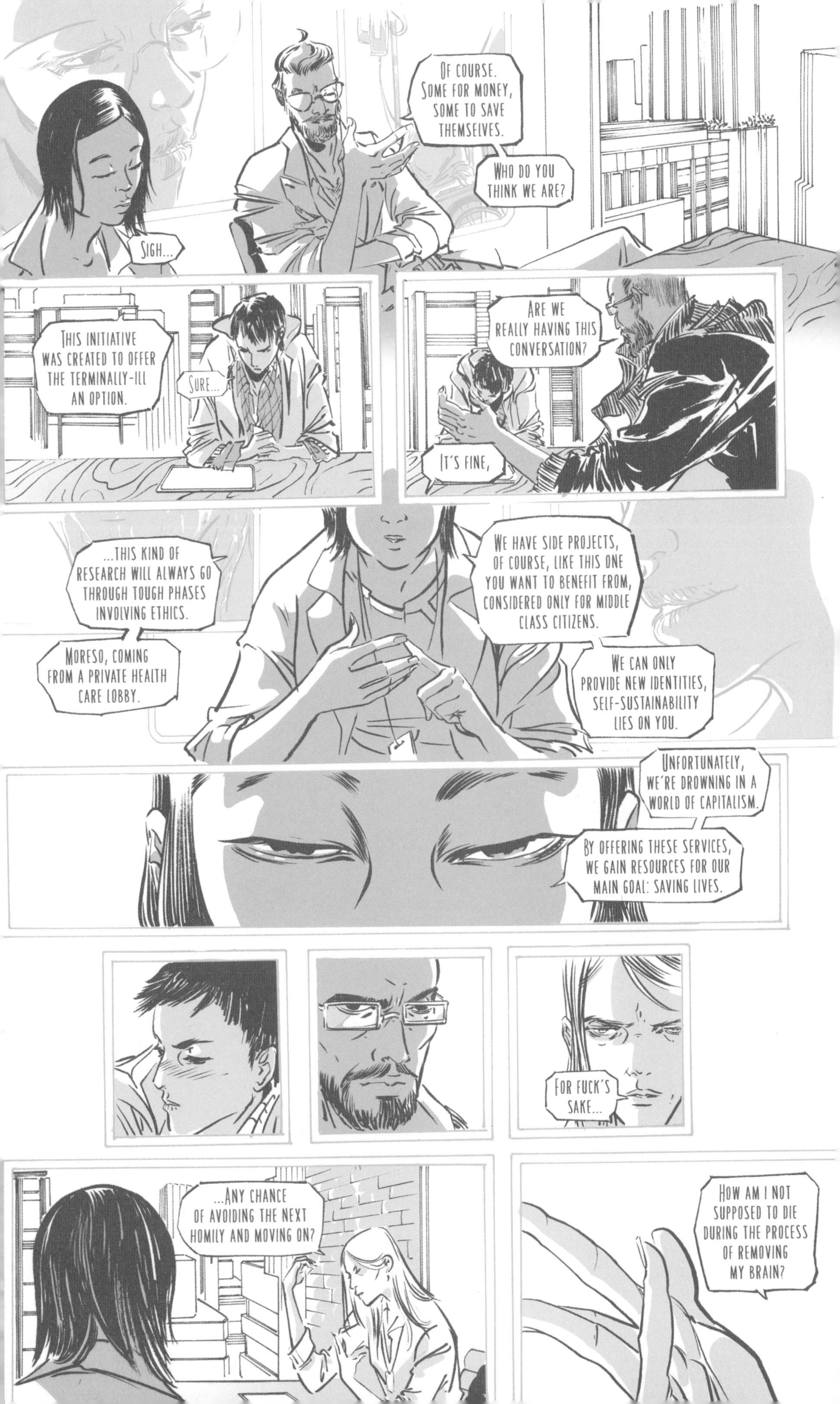

Of course. Some for money, some to save themselves.
Who do you think we are?
Sigh...
This initiative was created to offer the terminally-ill an option.
Sure...
Are we really having this conversation?
It's fine,
...this kind of research will always go through tough phases involving ethics.
Moreso, coming from a private health care lobby.
We have side projects, of course, like this one you want to benefit from, considered only for middle class citizens.
We can only provide new identities, self-sustainability lies on you.
Unfortunately, we're drowning in a world of capitalism.
By offering these services, we gain resources for our main goal: saving lives.
For fuck's sake...
...Any chance of avoiding the next homily and moving on?
How am I not supposed to die during the process of removing my brain?

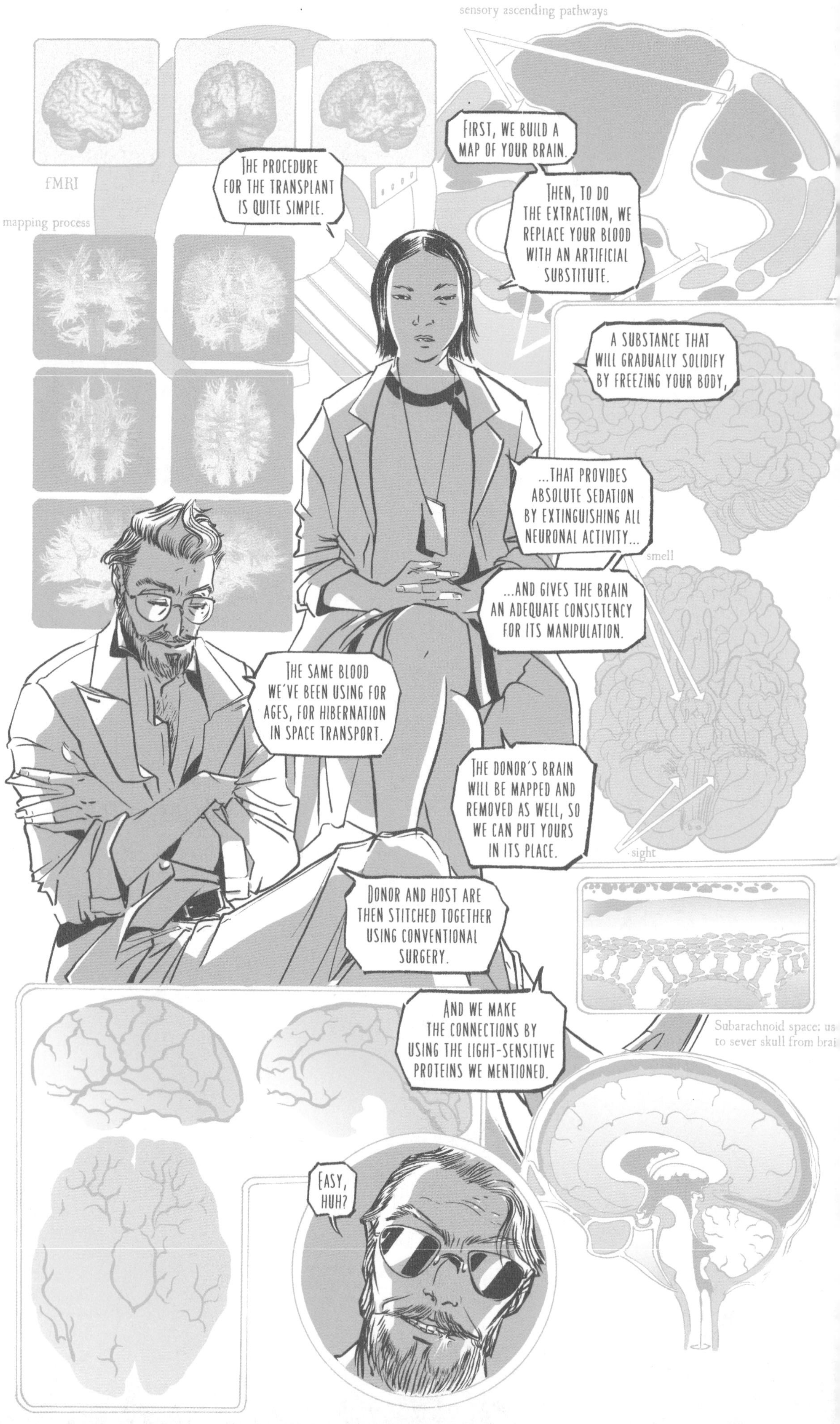

sensory ascending pathways
fMRI
mapping process
THE PROCEDURE FOR THE TRANSPLANT IS QUITE SIMPLE.
FIRST, WE BUILD A MAP OF YOUR BRAIN.
THEN, TO DO THE EXTRACTION, WE REPLACE YOUR BLOOD WITH AN ARTIFICIAL SUBSTITUTE.
A SUBSTANCE THAT WILL GRADUALLY SOLIDIFY BY FREEZING YOUR BODY,
...THAT PROVIDES ABSOLUTE SEDATION BY EXTINGUISHING ALL NEURONAL ACTIVITY...
...AND GIVES THE BRAIN AN ADEQUATE CONSISTENCY FOR ITS MANIPULATION.
smell
THE SAME BLOOD WE'VE BEEN USING FOR AGES, FOR HIBERNATION IN SPACE TRANSPORT.
THE DONOR'S BRAIN WILL BE MAPPED AND REMOVED AS WELL, SO WE CAN PUT YOURS IN ITS PLACE.
sight
DONOR AND HOST ARE THEN STITCHED TOGETHER USING CONVENTIONAL SURGERY.
AND WE MAKE THE CONNECTIONS BY USING THE LIGHT-SENSITIVE PROTEINS WE MENTIONED.
Subarachnoid space: us
to sever skull from brai
EASY, HUH?

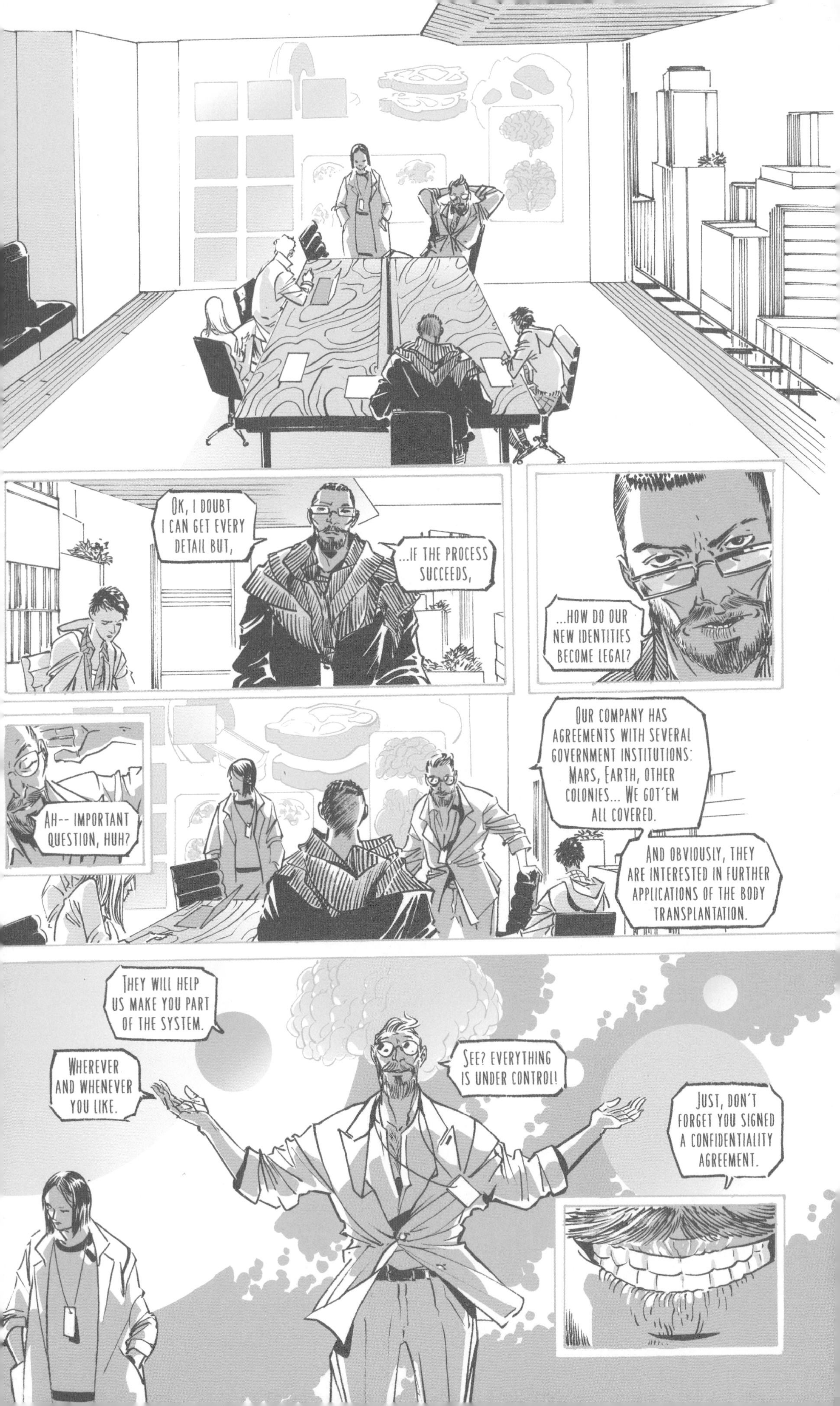

OK, I DOUBT I CAN GET EVERY DETAIL BUT,
...IF THE PROCESS SUCCEEDS,
...HOW DO OUR NEW IDENTITIES BECOME LEGAL?
AH-- IMPORTANT QUESTION, HUH?
OUR COMPANY HAS AGREEMENTS WITH SEVERAL GOVERNMENT INSTITUTIONS: MARS, EARTH, OTHER COLONIES... WE GOT'EM ALL COVERED.
AND OBVIOUSLY, THEY ARE INTERESTED IN FURTHER APPLICATIONS OF THE BODY TRANSPLANTATION.
THEY WILL HELP US MAKE YOU PART OF THE SYSTEM.
WHEREVER AND WHENEVER YOU LIKE.
SEE? EVERYTHING IS UNDER CONTROL!
JUST, DON'T FORGET YOU SIGNED A CONFIDENTIALITY AGREEMENT.

Chapter 4: Chez Charlotte

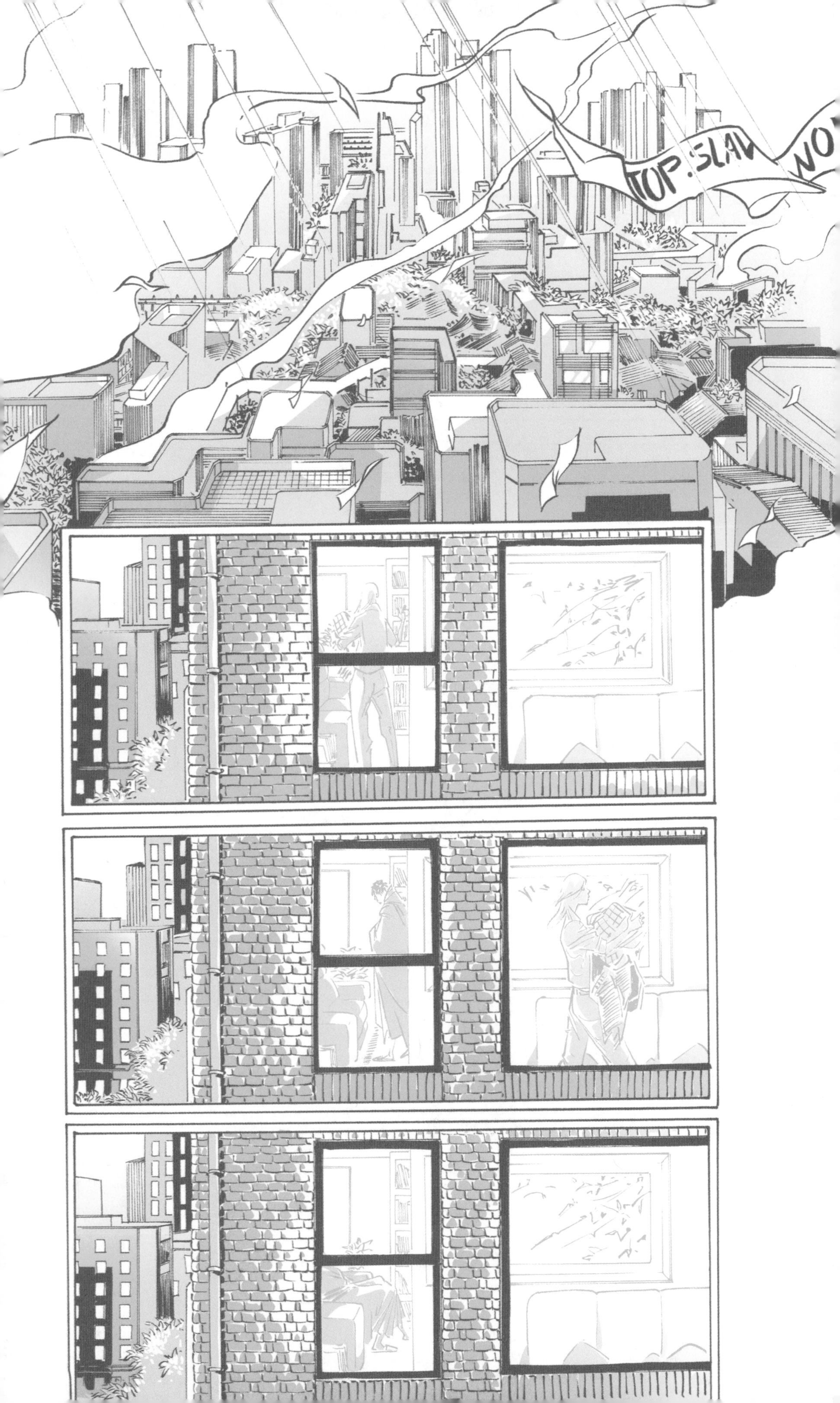
TOP · SLAV
NO

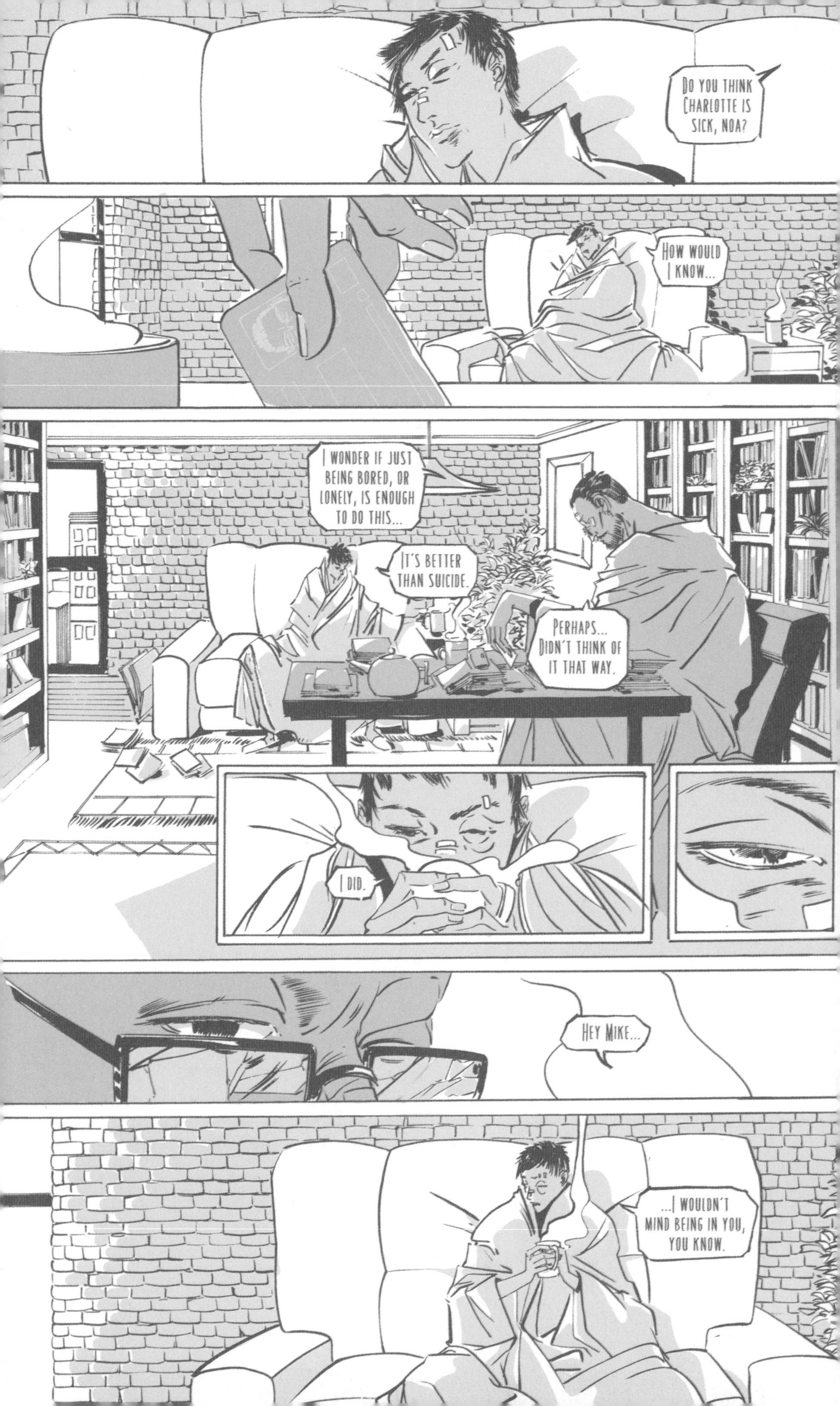

Do you think Charlotte is sick, Noa?
How would I know...
I wonder if just being bored, or lonely, is enough to do this...
It's better than suicide.
Perhaps... Didn't think of it that way.
I did.
Hey Mike...
...I wouldn't mind being in you, you know.

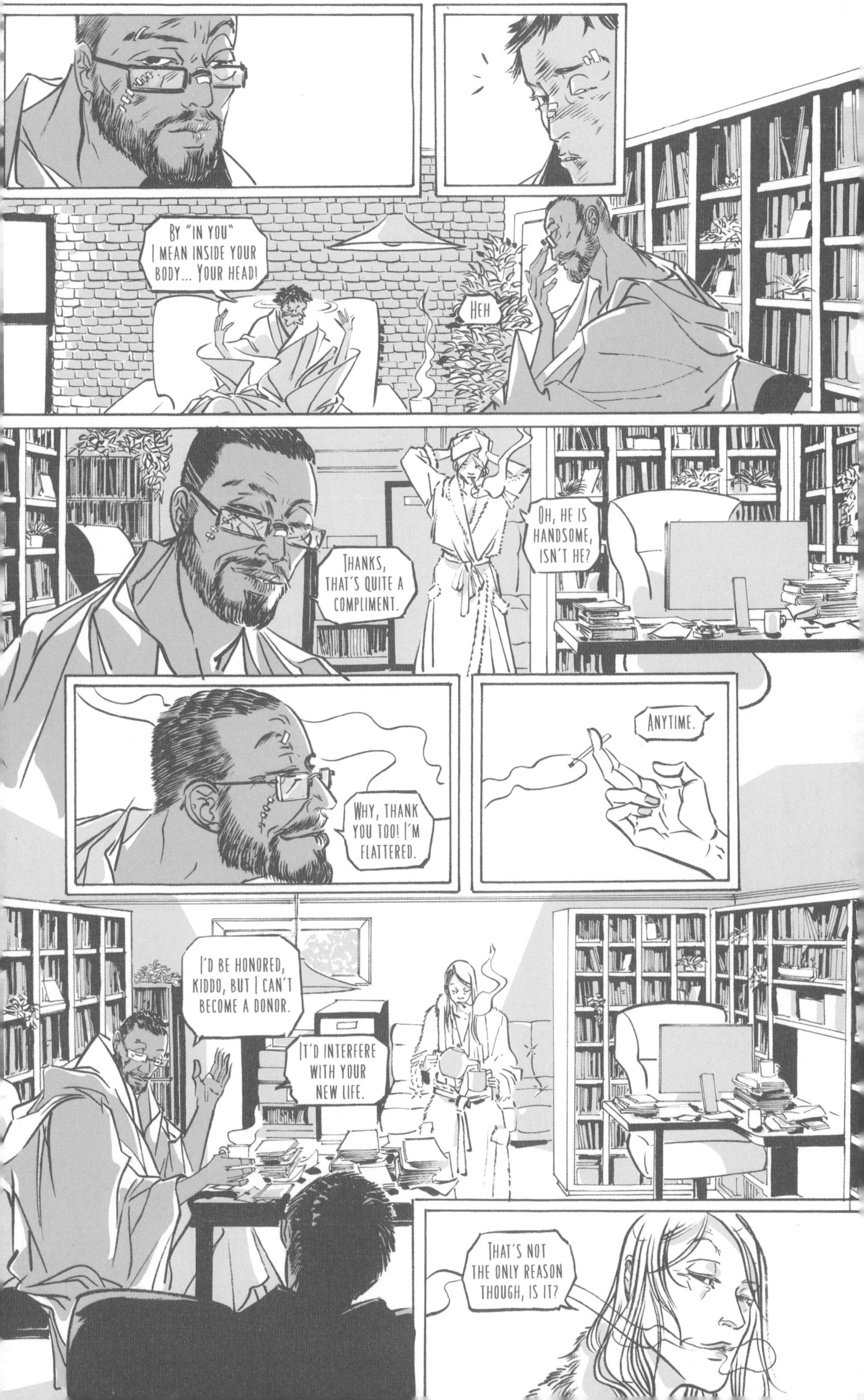
BY "IN YOU" I MEAN INSIDE YOUR BODY... YOUR HEAD!
HEH
THANKS, THAT'S QUITE A COMPLIMENT.
OH, HE IS HANDSOME, ISN'T HE?
WHY, THANK YOU TOO! I'M FLATTERED.
ANYTIME.
I'D BE HONORED, KIDDO, BUT I CAN'T BECOME A DONOR.
IT'D INTERFERE WITH YOUR NEW LIFE.
THAT'S NOT THE ONLY REASON THOUGH, IS IT?

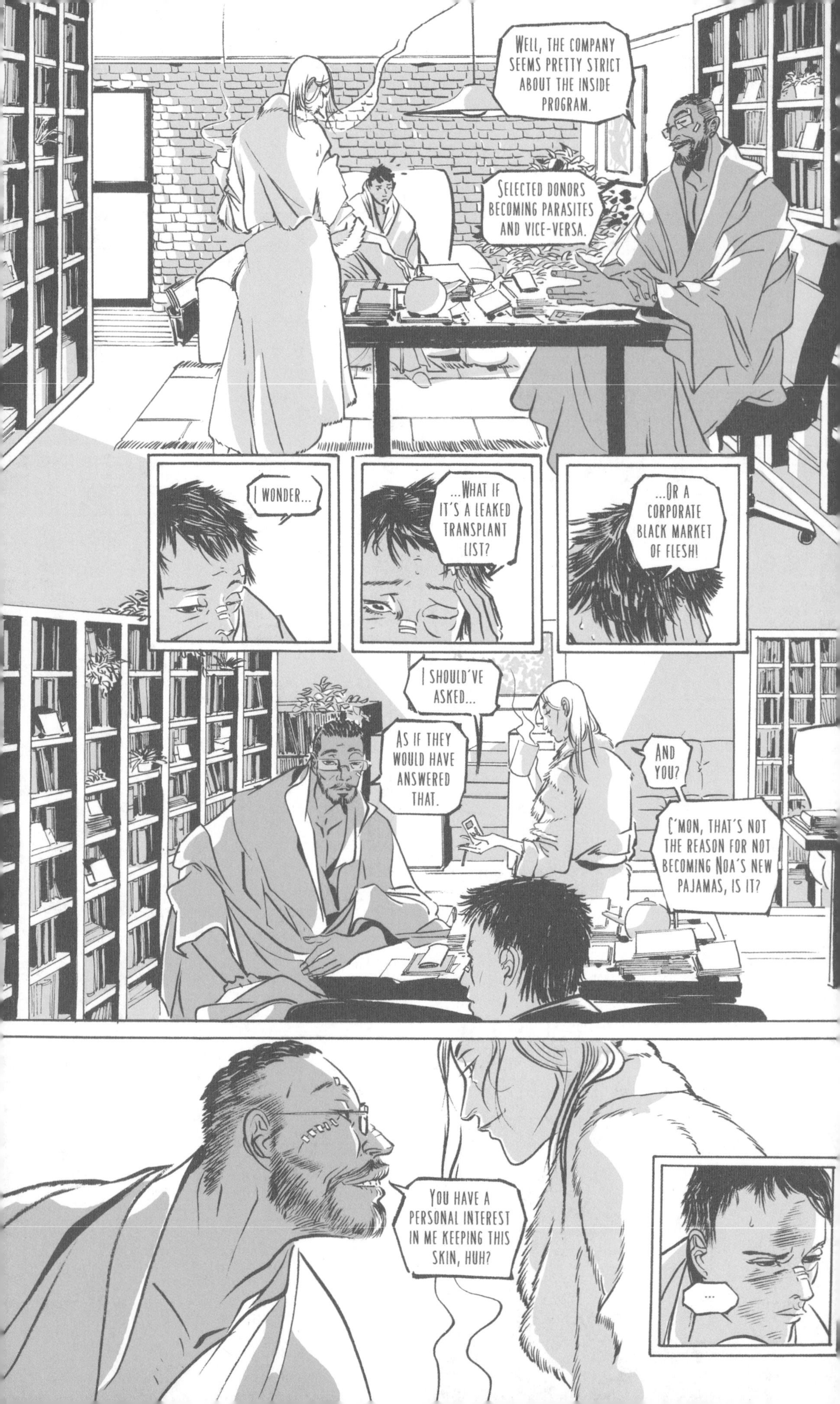
Well, the company seems pretty strict about the inside program.
Selected donors becoming parasites and vice-versa.
I wonder...
...What if it's a leaked transplant list?
...Or a corporate black market of flesh!
I should've asked...
As if they would have answered that.
And you?
C'mon, that's not the reason for not becoming Noa's new pajamas, is it?
You have a personal interest in me keeping this skin, huh?
...

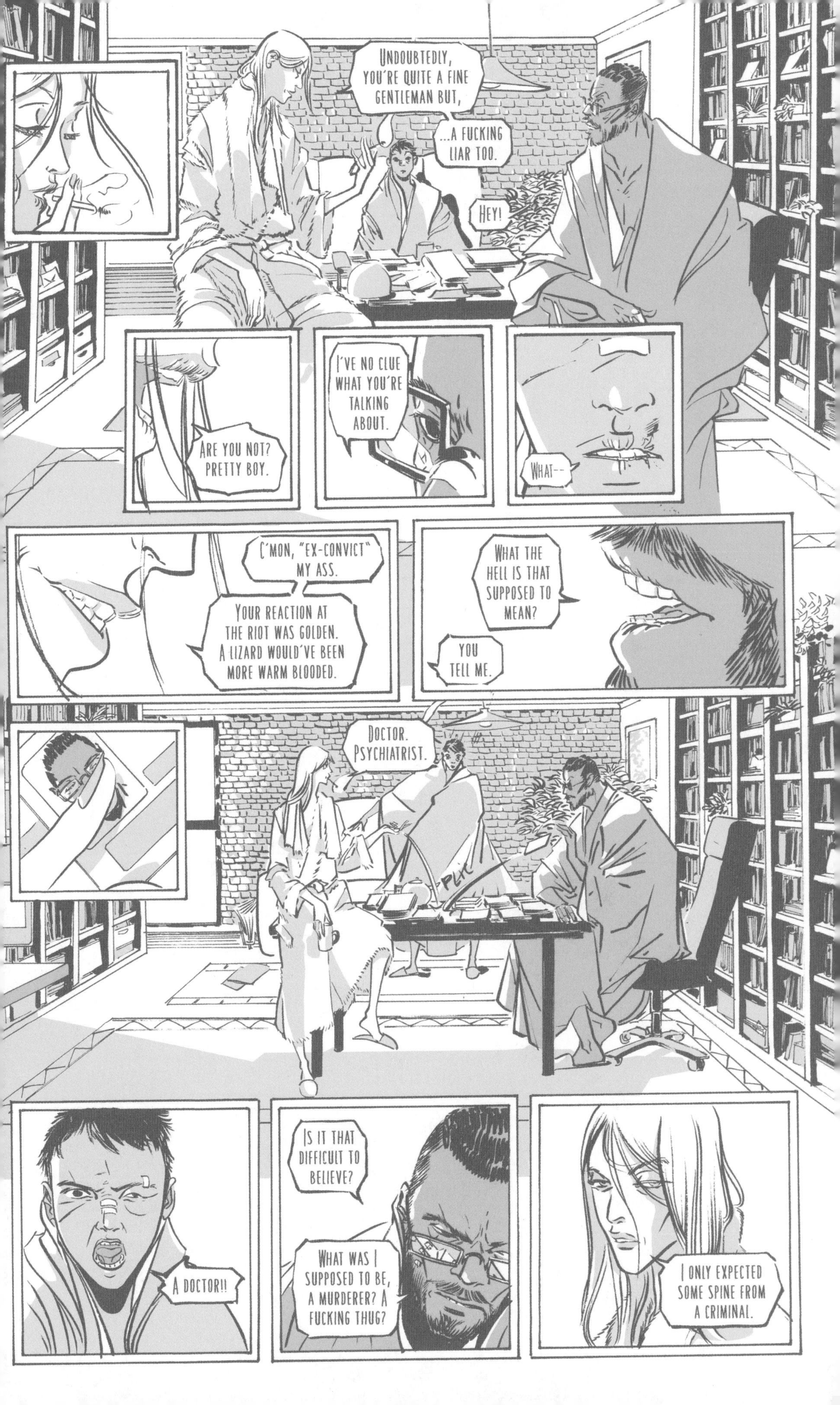
UNDOUBTEDLY, YOU'RE QUITE A FINE GENTLEMAN BUT,
...A FUCKING LIAR TOO.
HEY!
ARE YOU NOT? PRETTY BOY.
I'VE NO CLUE WHAT YOU'RE TALKING ABOUT.
WHAT--
C'MON, "EX-CONVICT" MY ASS.
YOUR REACTION AT THE RIOT WAS GOLDEN. A LIZARD WOULD'VE BEEN MORE WARM BLOODED.
WHAT THE HELL IS THAT SUPPOSED TO MEAN?
YOU TELL ME.
DOCTOR. PSYCHIATRIST.
PLIC
A DOCTOR!!
IS IT THAT DIFFICULT TO BELIEVE?
WHAT WAS I SUPPOSED TO BE, A MURDERER? A FUCKING THUG?
I ONLY EXPECTED SOME SPINE FROM A CRIMINAL.

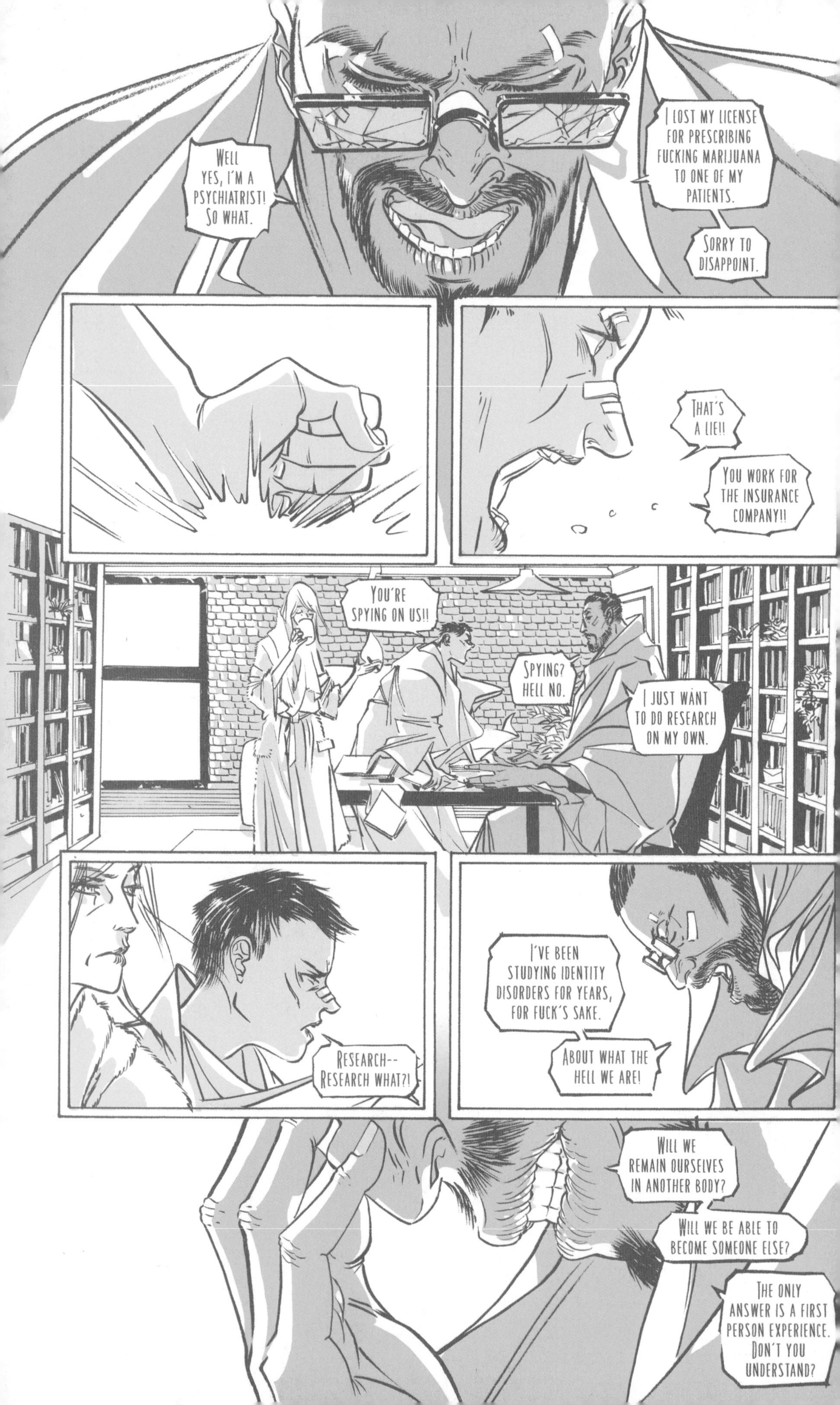

WELL YES, I'M A PSYCHIATRIST! SO WHAT.
I LOST MY LICENSE FOR PRESCRIBING FUCKING MARIJUANA TO ONE OF MY PATIENTS.
SORRY TO DISAPPOINT.
THAT'S A LIE!!
YOU WORK FOR THE INSURANCE COMPANY!!
YOU'RE SPYING ON US!!
SPYING? HELL NO.
I JUST WANT TO DO RESEARCH ON MY OWN.
RESEARCH-- RESEARCH WHAT?!
I'VE BEEN STUDYING IDENTITY DISORDERS FOR YEARS, FOR FUCK'S SAKE.
ABOUT WHAT THE HELL WE ARE!
WILL WE REMAIN OURSELVES IN ANOTHER BODY?
WILL WE BE ABLE TO BECOME SOMEONE ELSE?
THE ONLY ANSWER IS A FIRST PERSON EXPERIENCE. DON'T YOU UNDERSTAND?

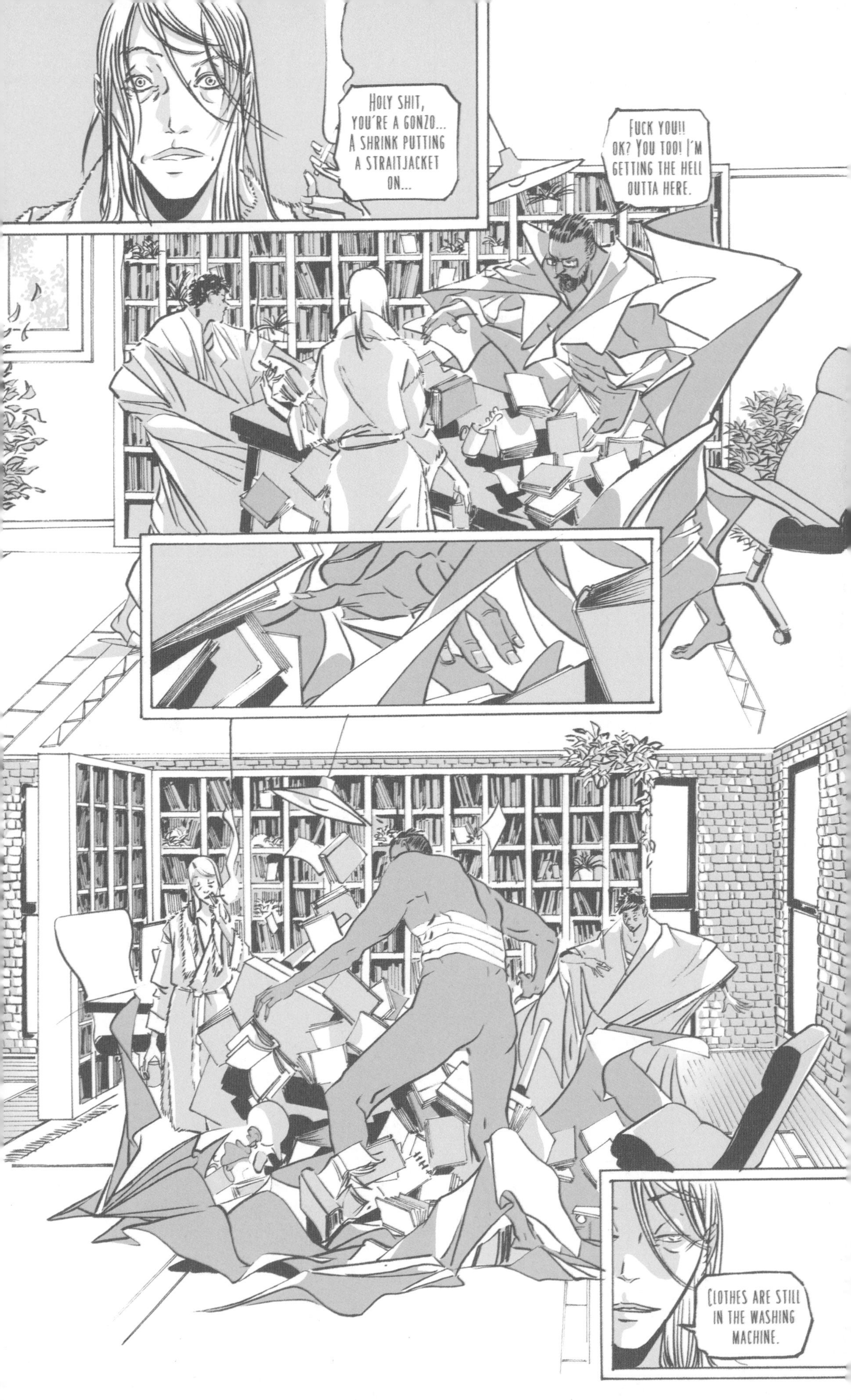
HOLY SHIT, YOU'RE A GONZO... A SHRINK PUTTING A STRAITJACKET ON...
FUCK YOU!! OK? YOU TOO! I'M GETTING THE HELL OUTTA HERE.
CLOTHES ARE STILL IN THE WASHING MACHINE.

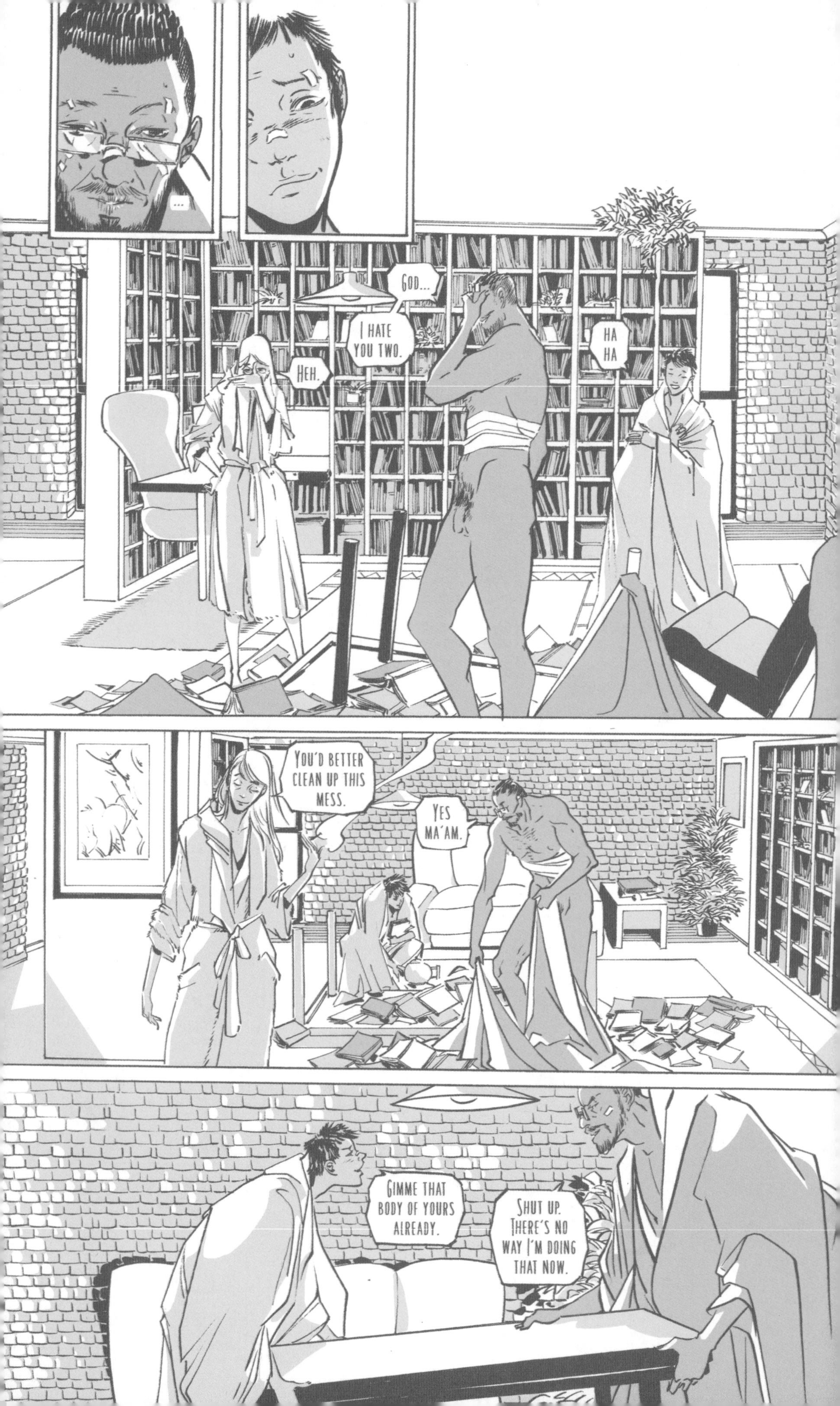
...
GOD...
I HATE YOU TWO.
HEH.
HA HA
YOU'D BETTER CLEAN UP THIS MESS.
YES MA'AM.
GIMME THAT BODY OF YOURS ALREADY.
SHUT UP. THERE'S NO WAY I'M DOING THAT NOW.

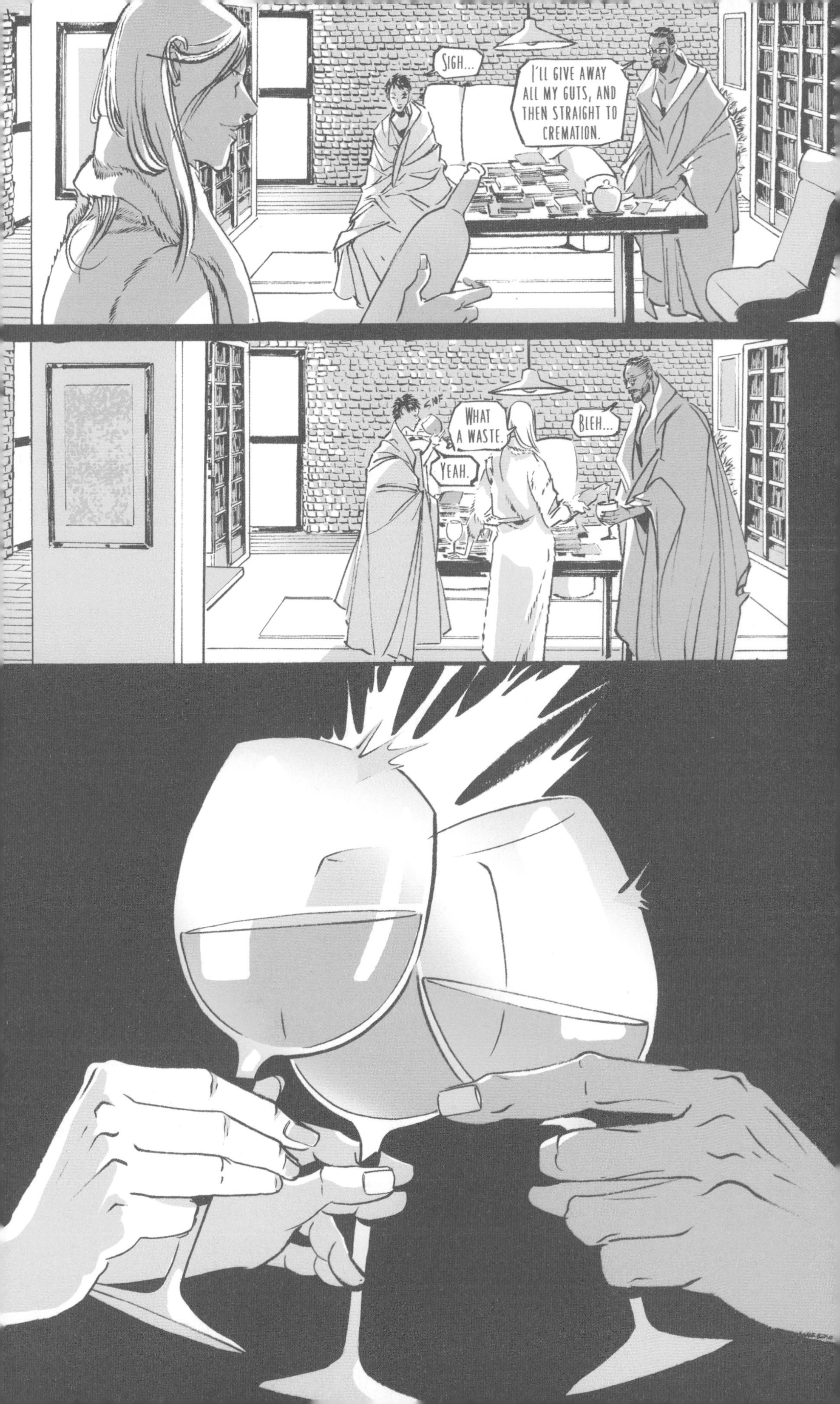
SIGH...
I'LL GIVE AWAY ALL MY GUTS, AND THEN STRAIGHT TO CREMATION.
SNF
WHAT A WASTE.
YEAH.
BLEH...

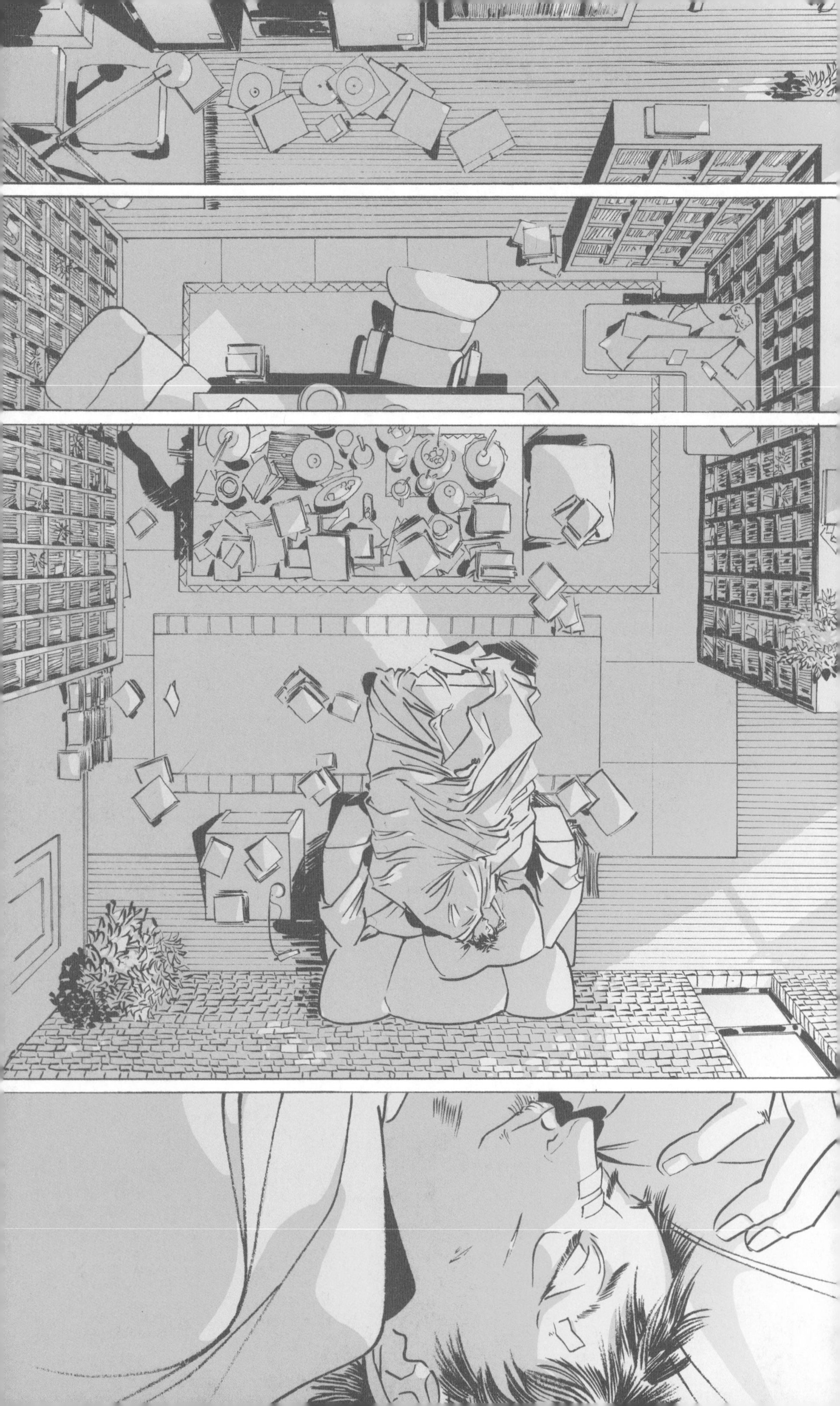

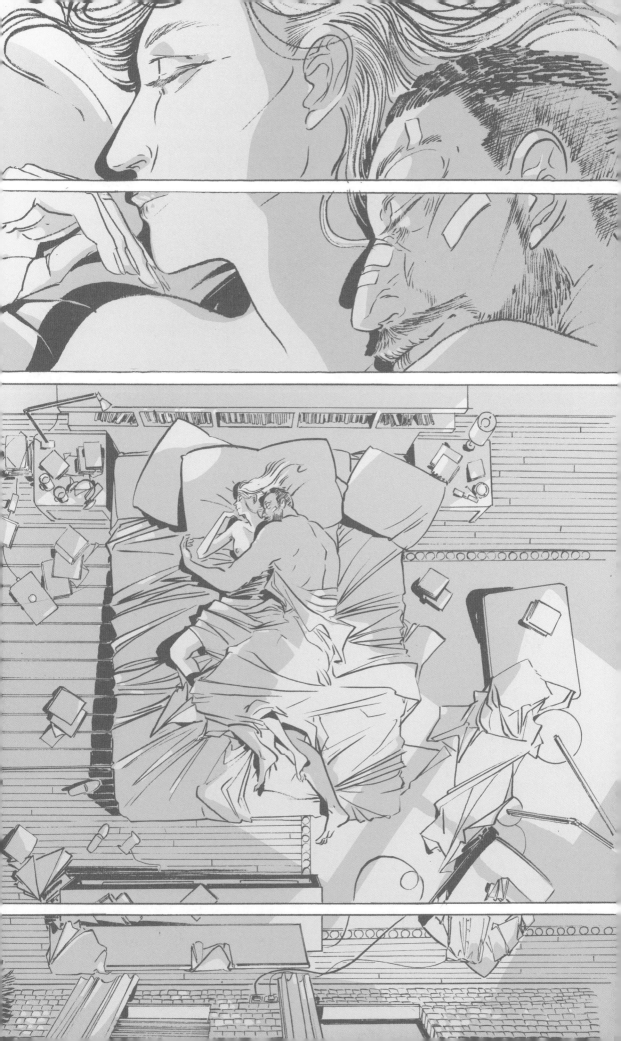

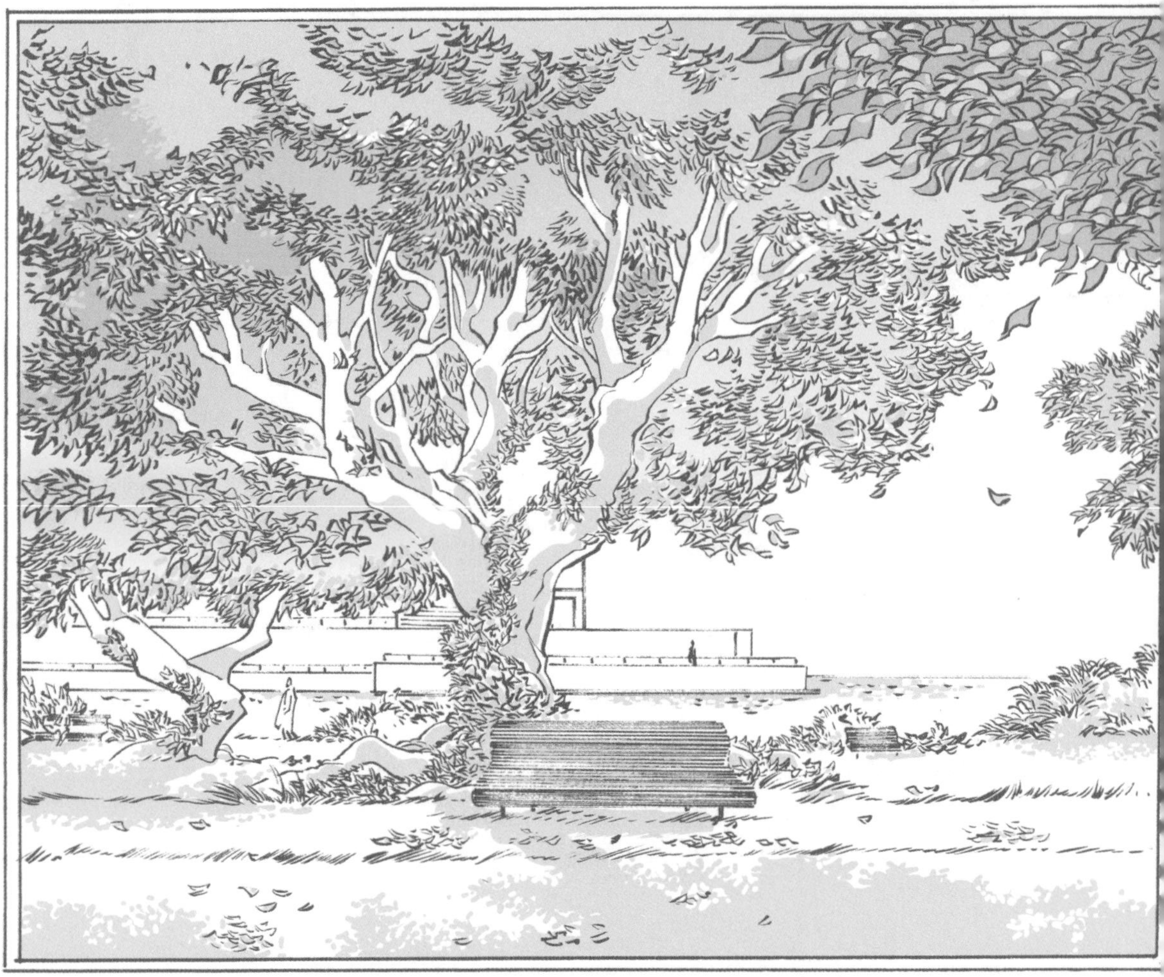
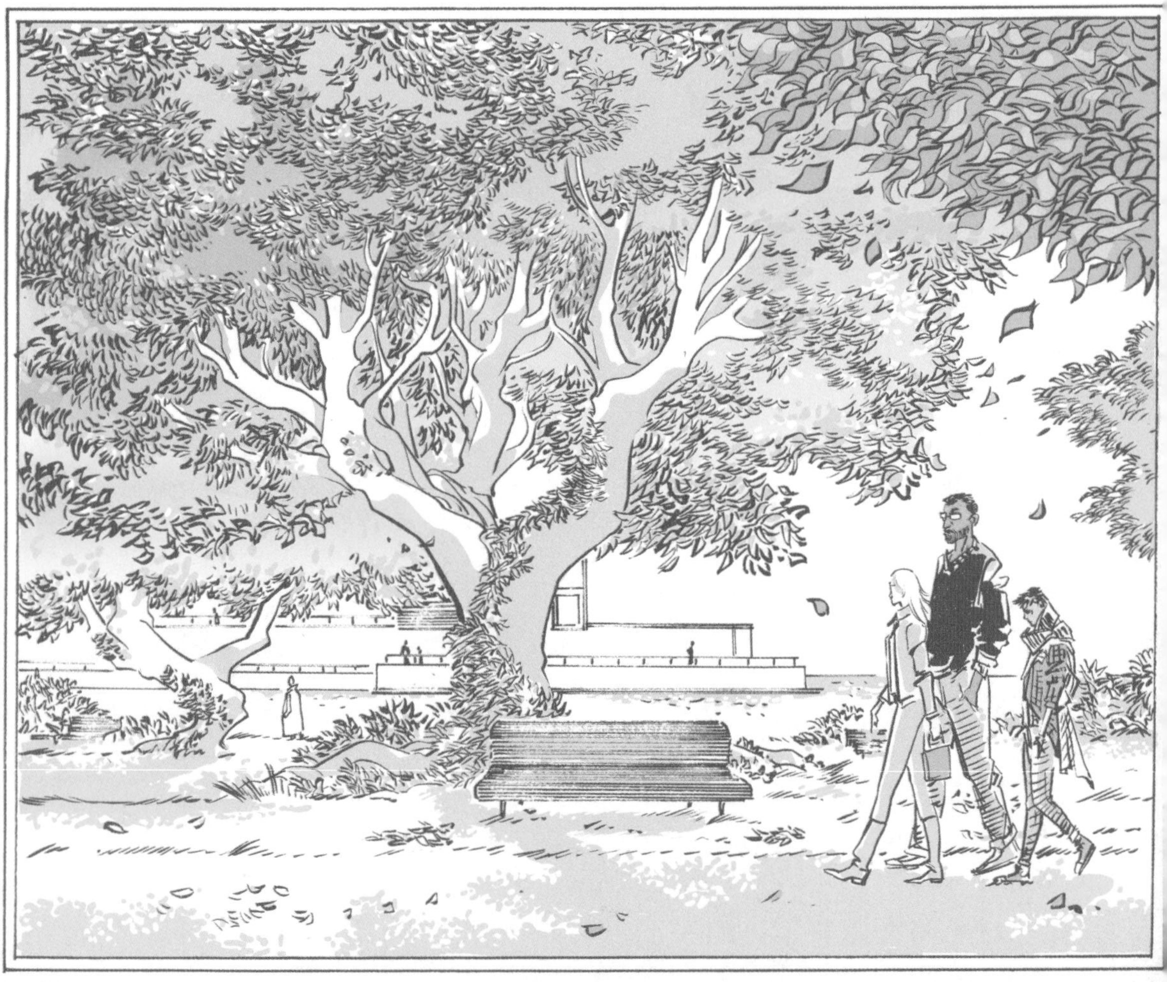

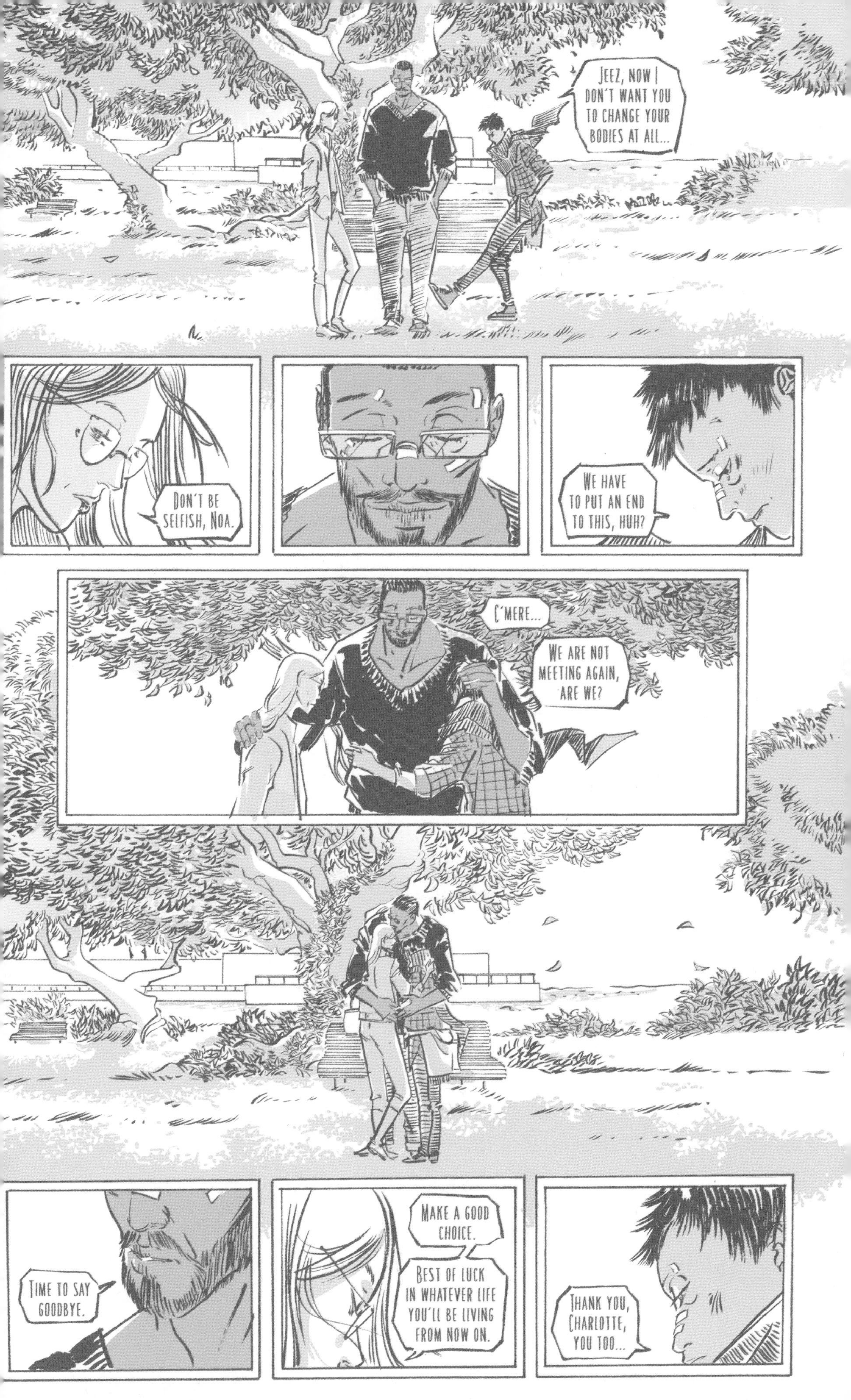
JEEZ, NOW I DON'T WANT YOU TO CHANGE YOUR BODIES AT ALL...
DON'T BE SELFISH, NOA.
WE HAVE TO PUT AN END TO THIS, HUH?
C'MERE...
WE ARE NOT MEETING AGAIN, ARE WE?
TIME TO SAY GOODBYE.
MAKE A GOOD CHOICE.
BEST OF LUCK IN WHATEVER LIFE YOU'LL BE LIVING FROM NOW ON.
THANK YOU, CHARLOTTE, YOU TOO...

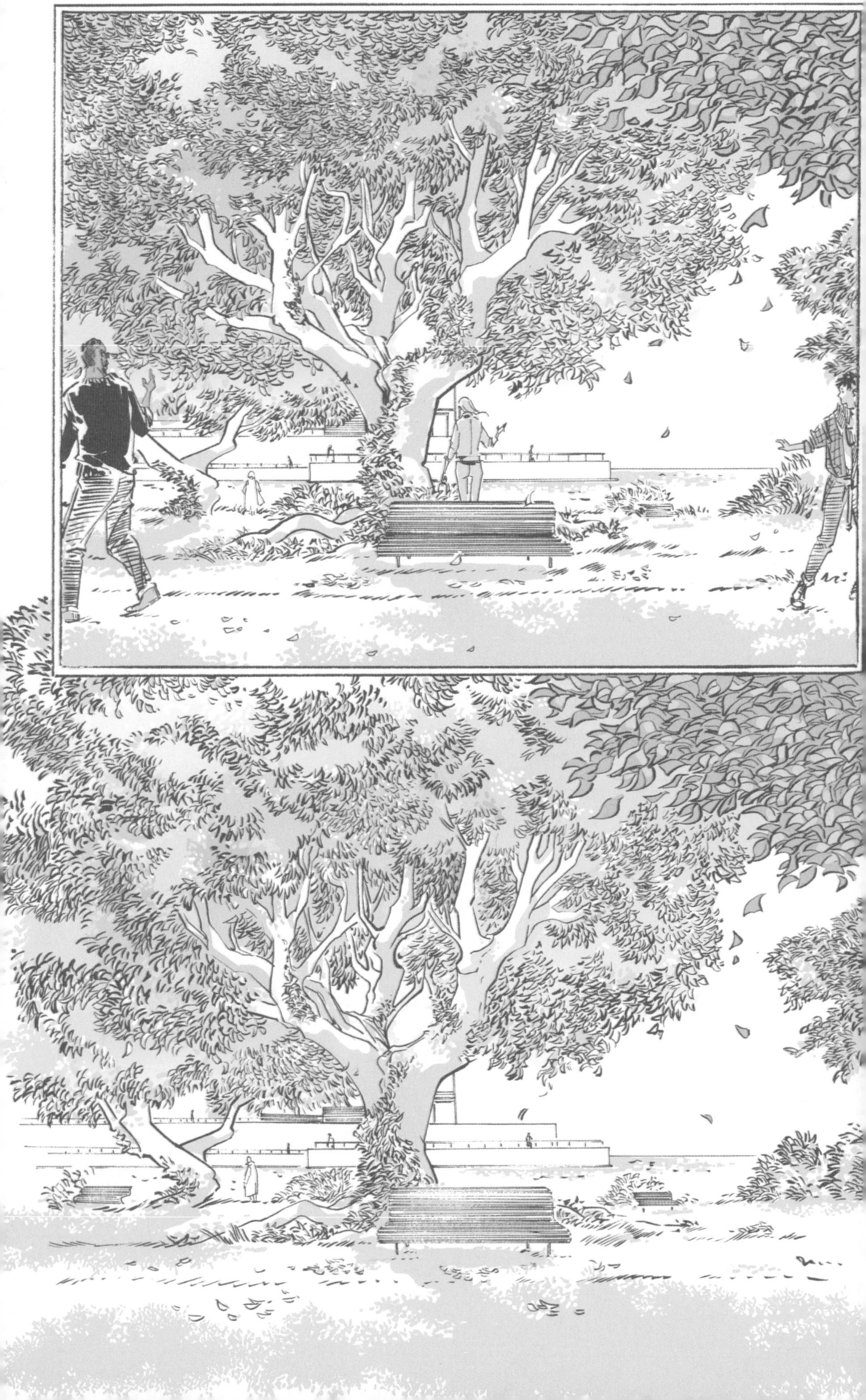

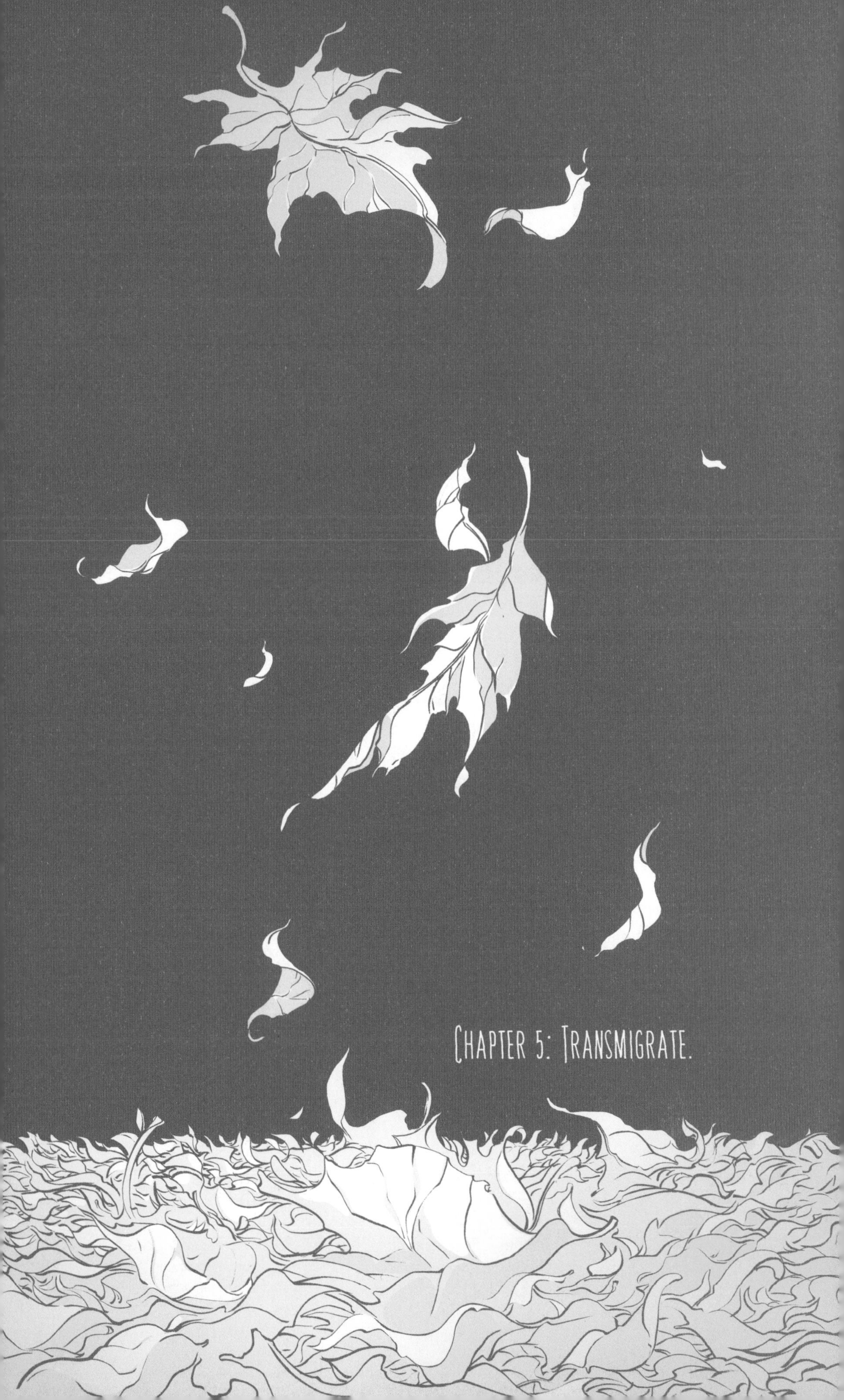

Chapter 5: Transmigrate.

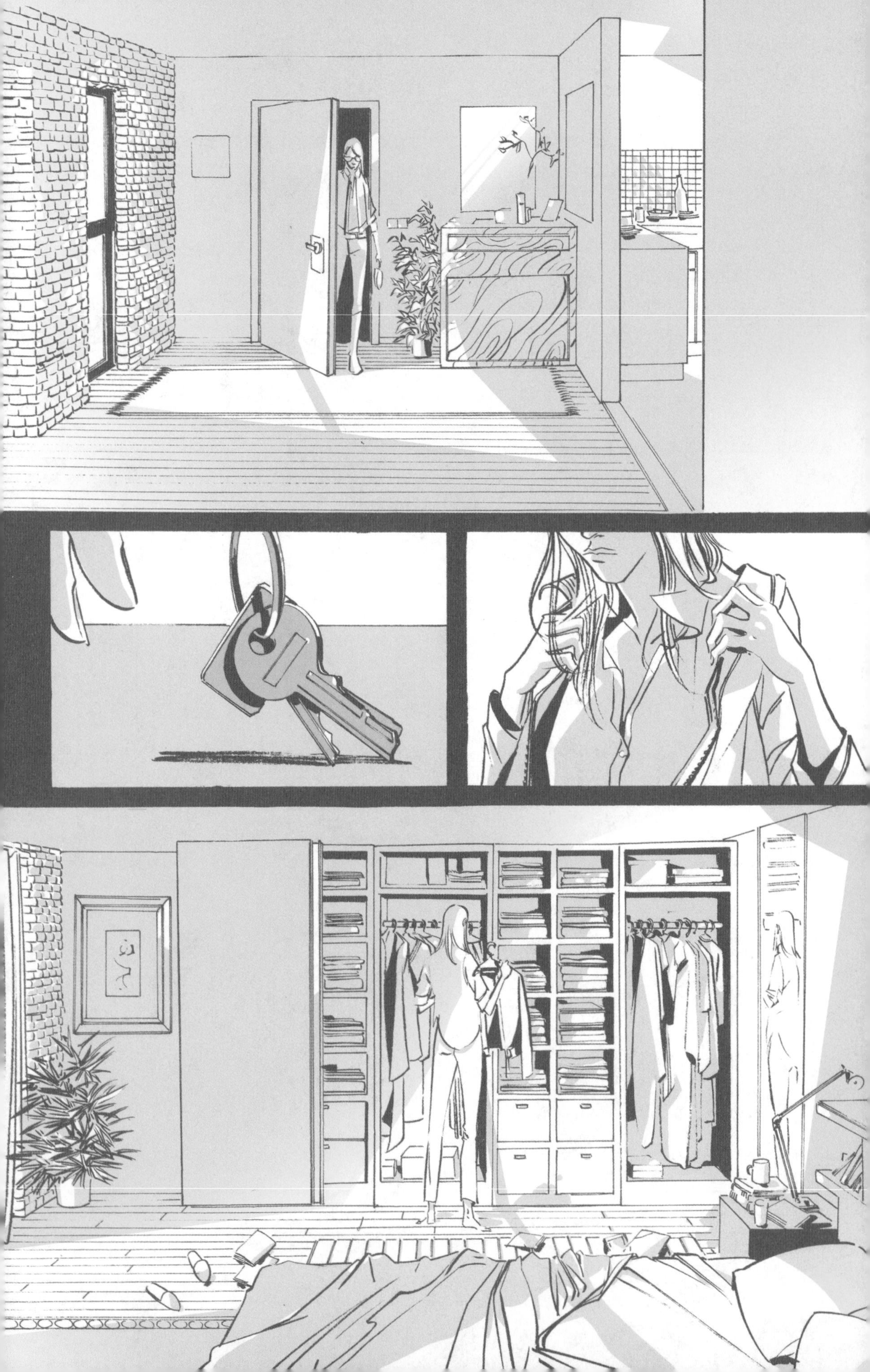

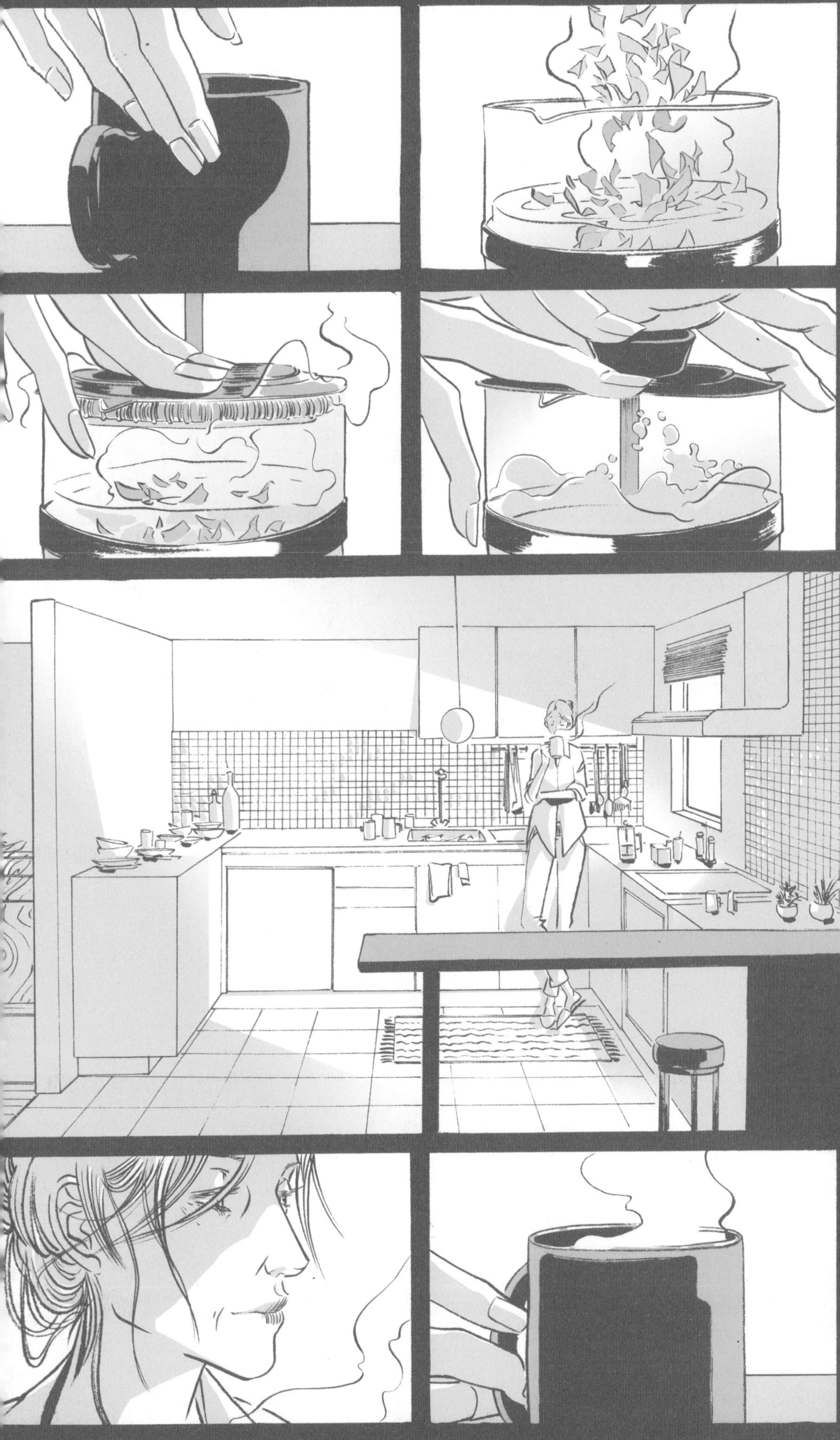

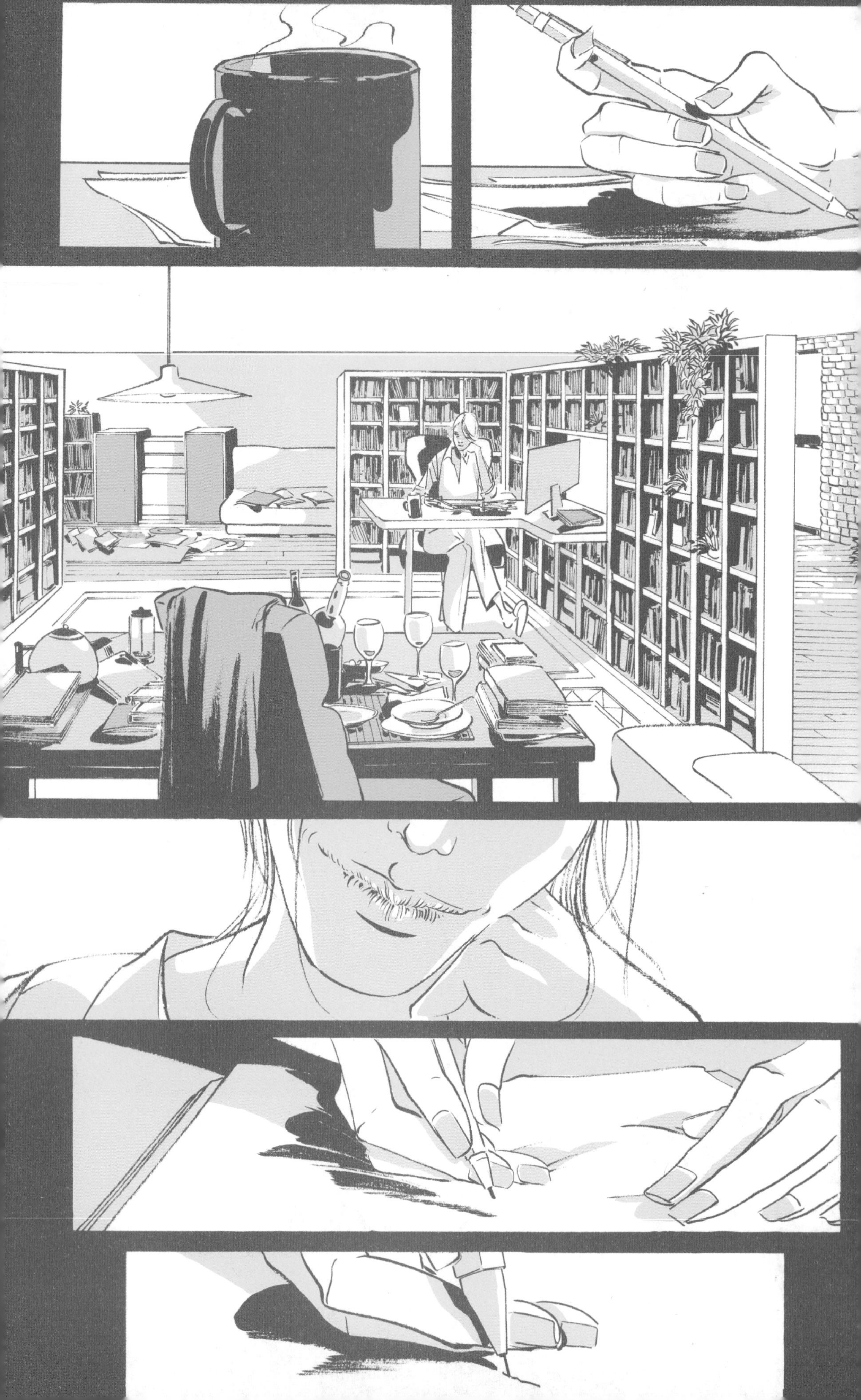

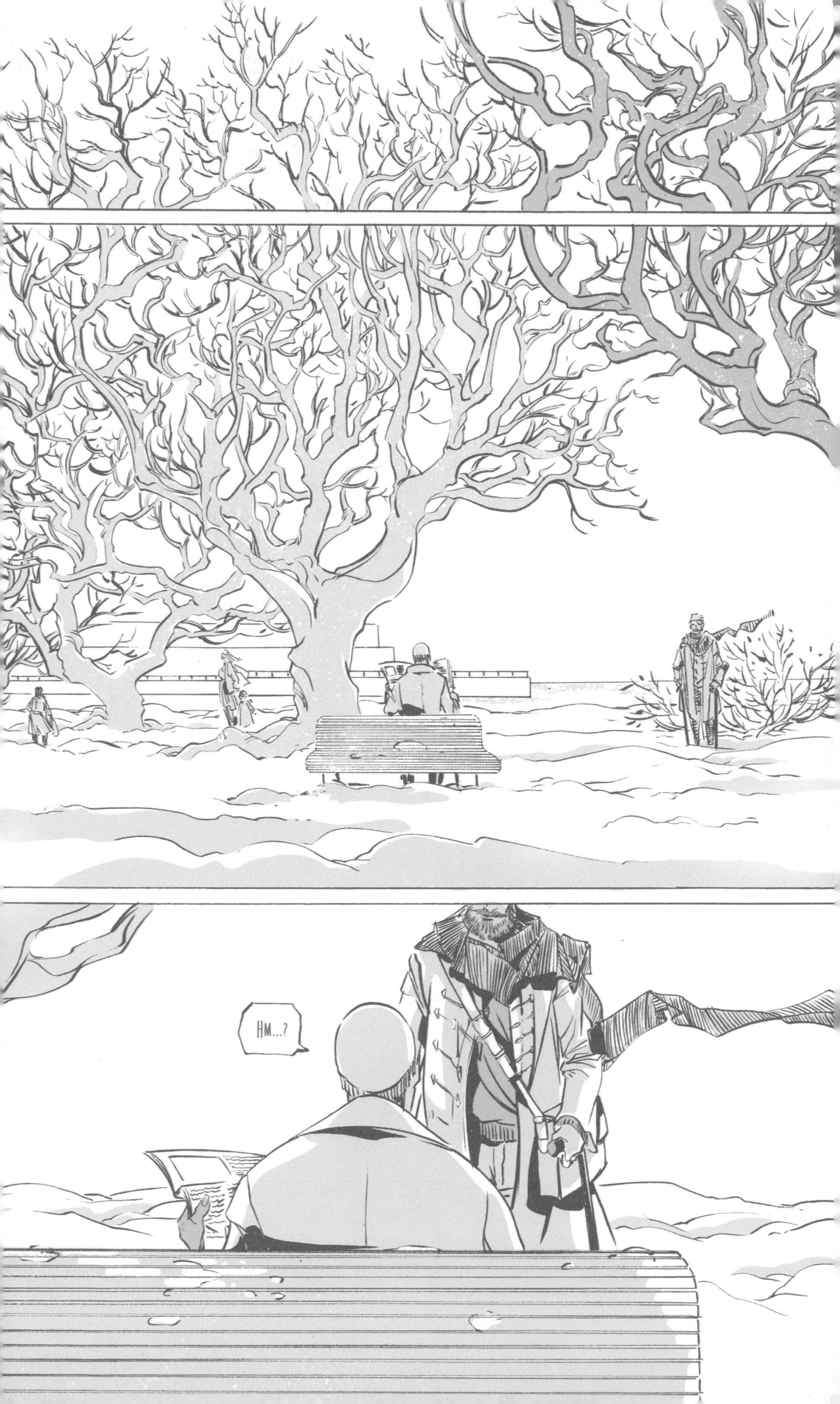
HM...?

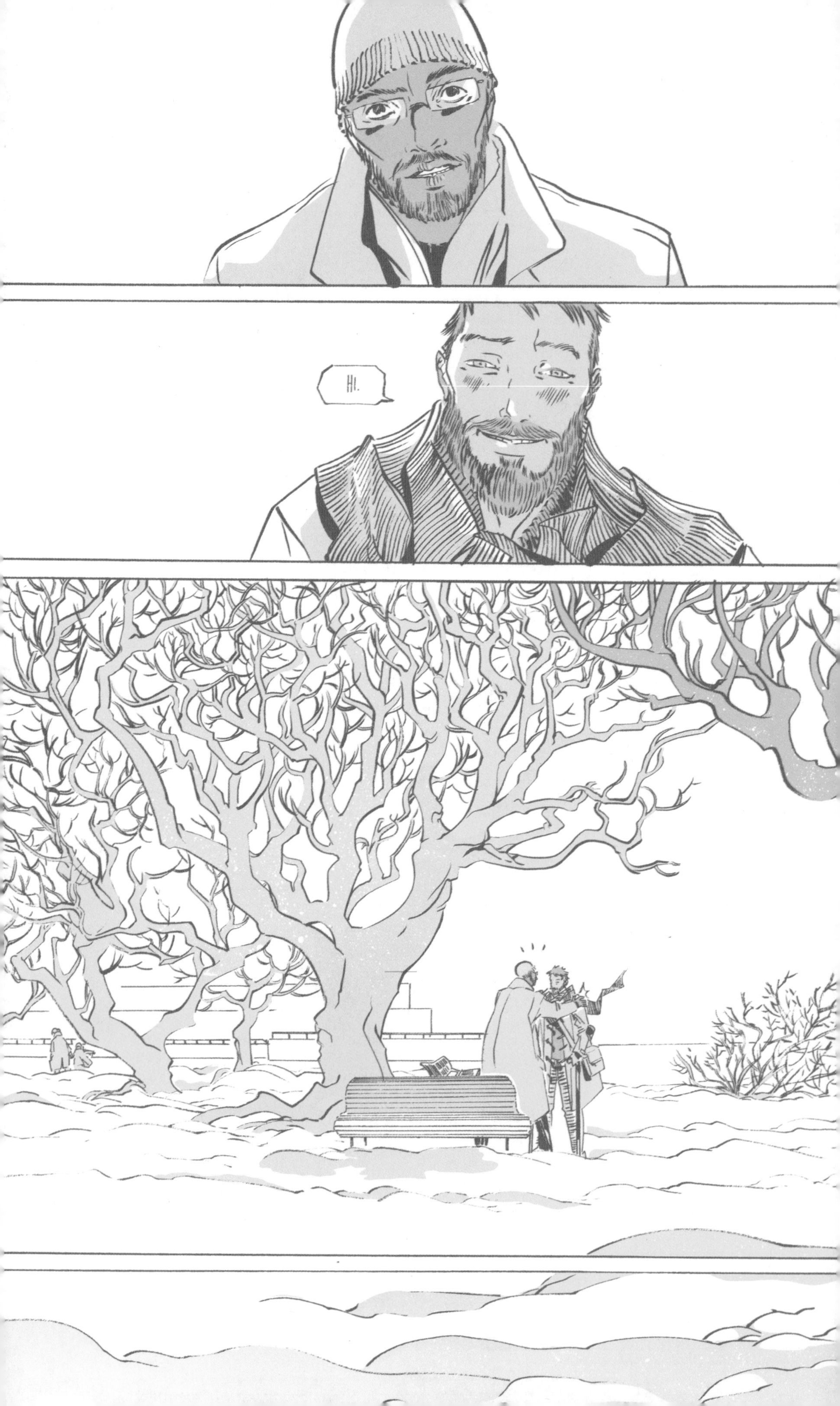
HI.

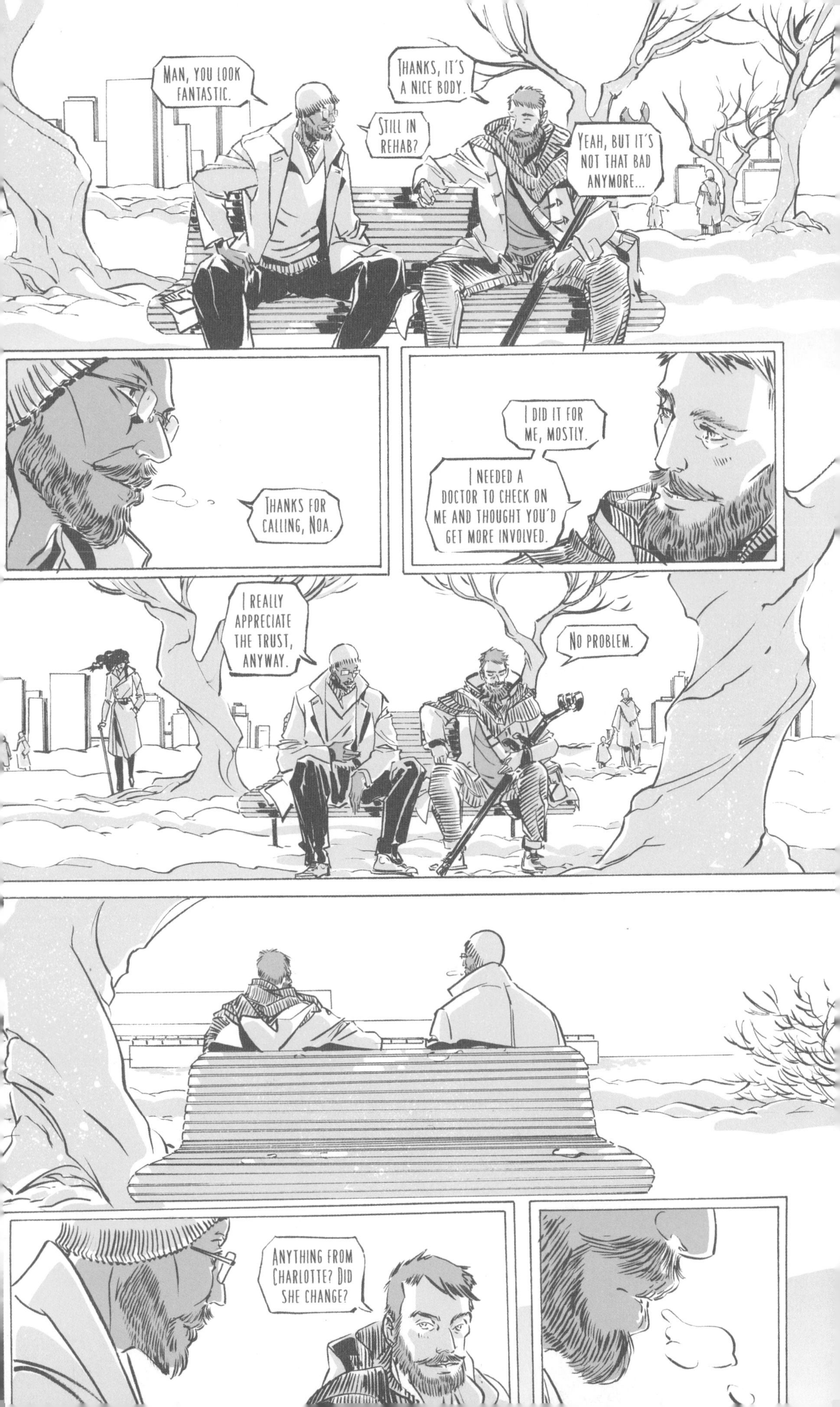

MAN, YOU LOOK FANTASTIC.
THANKS, IT'S A NICE BODY.
STILL IN REHAB?
YEAH, BUT IT'S NOT THAT BAD ANYMORE...
THANKS FOR CALLING, NOA.
I DID IT FOR ME, MOSTLY.
I NEEDED A DOCTOR TO CHECK ON ME AND THOUGHT YOU'D GET MORE INVOLVED.
I REALLY APPRECIATE THE TRUST, ANYWAY.
NO PROBLEM.
ANYTHING FROM CHARLOTTE? DID SHE CHANGE?

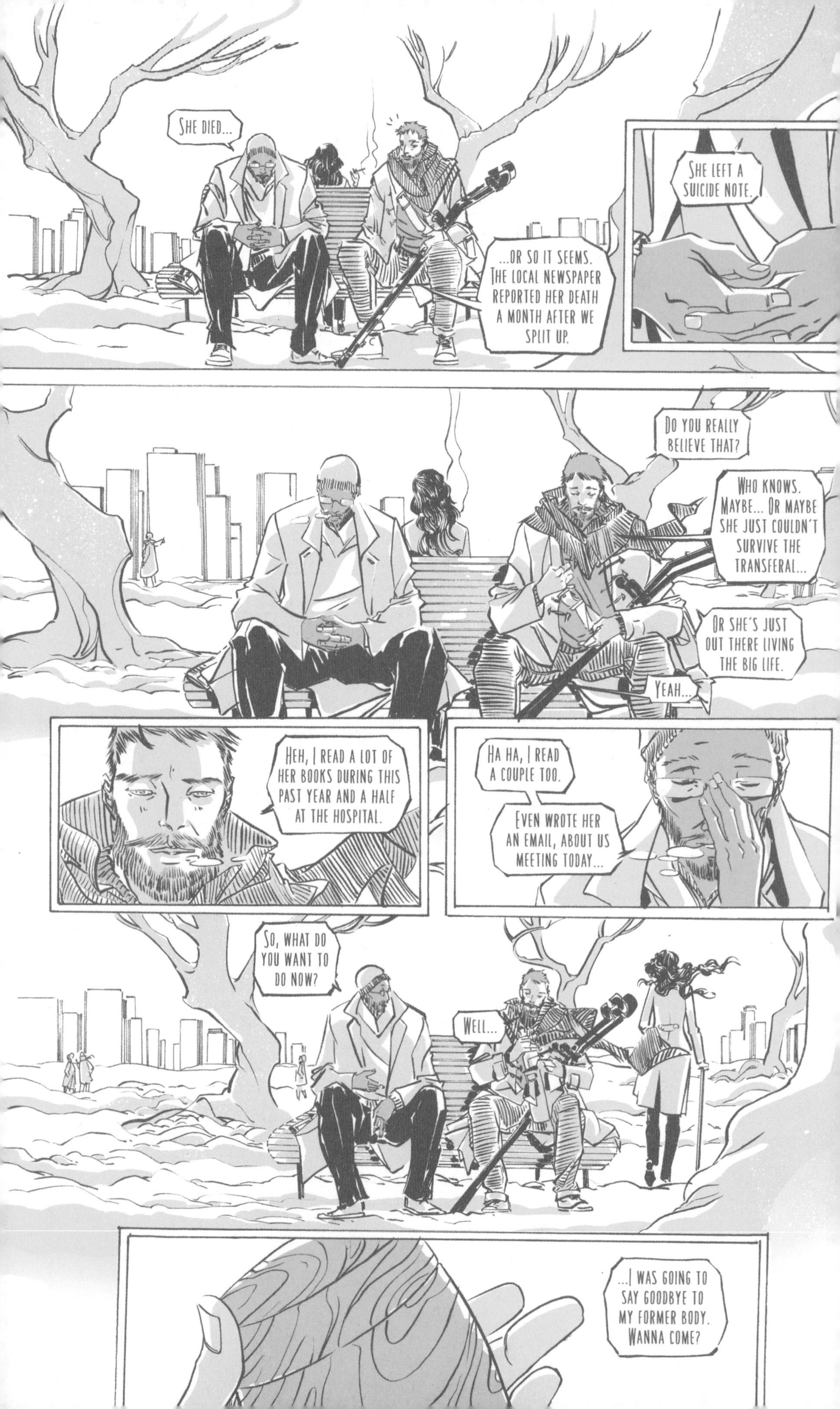
SHE DIED...
...OR SO IT SEEMS. THE LOCAL NEWSPAPER REPORTED HER DEATH A MONTH AFTER WE SPLIT UP.
SHE LEFT A SUICIDE NOTE.
DO YOU REALLY BELIEVE THAT?
WHO KNOWS. MAYBE... OR MAYBE SHE JUST COULDN'T SURVIVE THE TRANSFERAL...
OR SHE'S JUST OUT THERE LIVING THE BIG LIFE.
YEAH...
HEH, I READ A LOT OF HER BOOKS DURING THIS PAST YEAR AND A HALF AT THE HOSPITAL.
HA HA, I READ A COUPLE TOO.
EVEN WROTE HER AN EMAIL, ABOUT US MEETING TODAY...
SO, WHAT DO YOU WANT TO DO NOW?
WELL...
...I WAS GOING TO SAY GOODBYE TO MY FORMER BODY. WANNA COME?

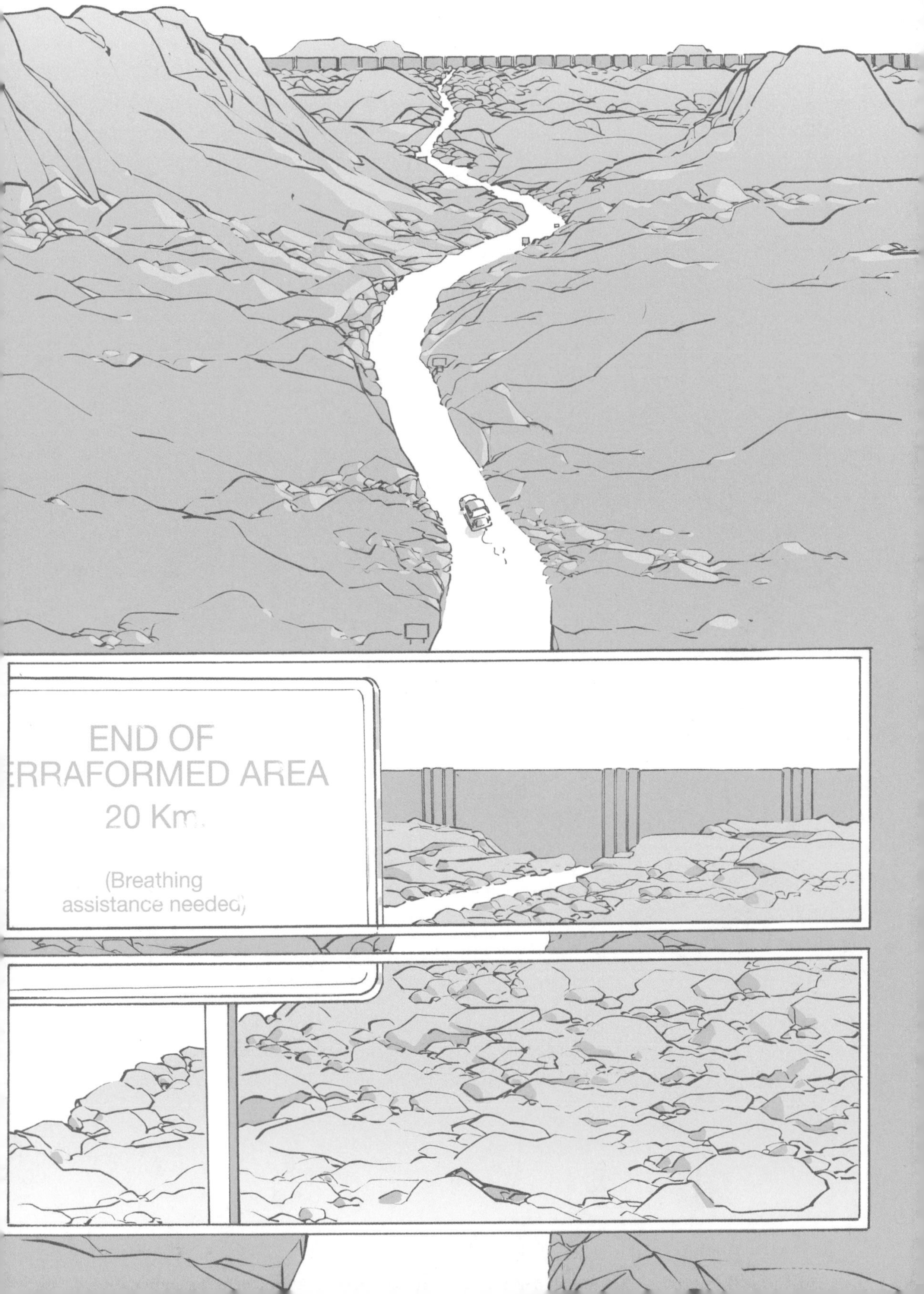
END OF
ERRAFORMED AREA
20 Km.
(Breathing
assistance needed)

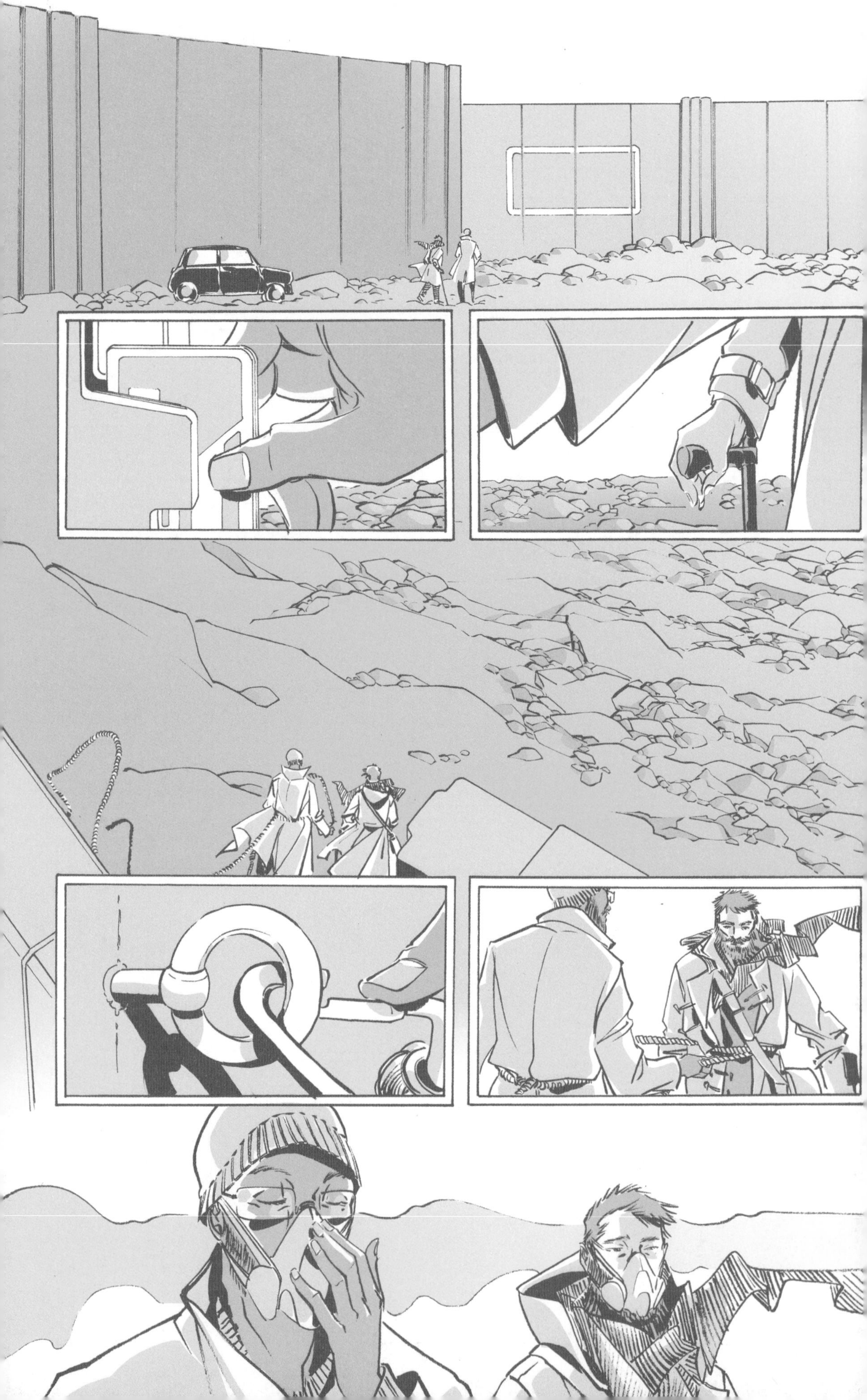

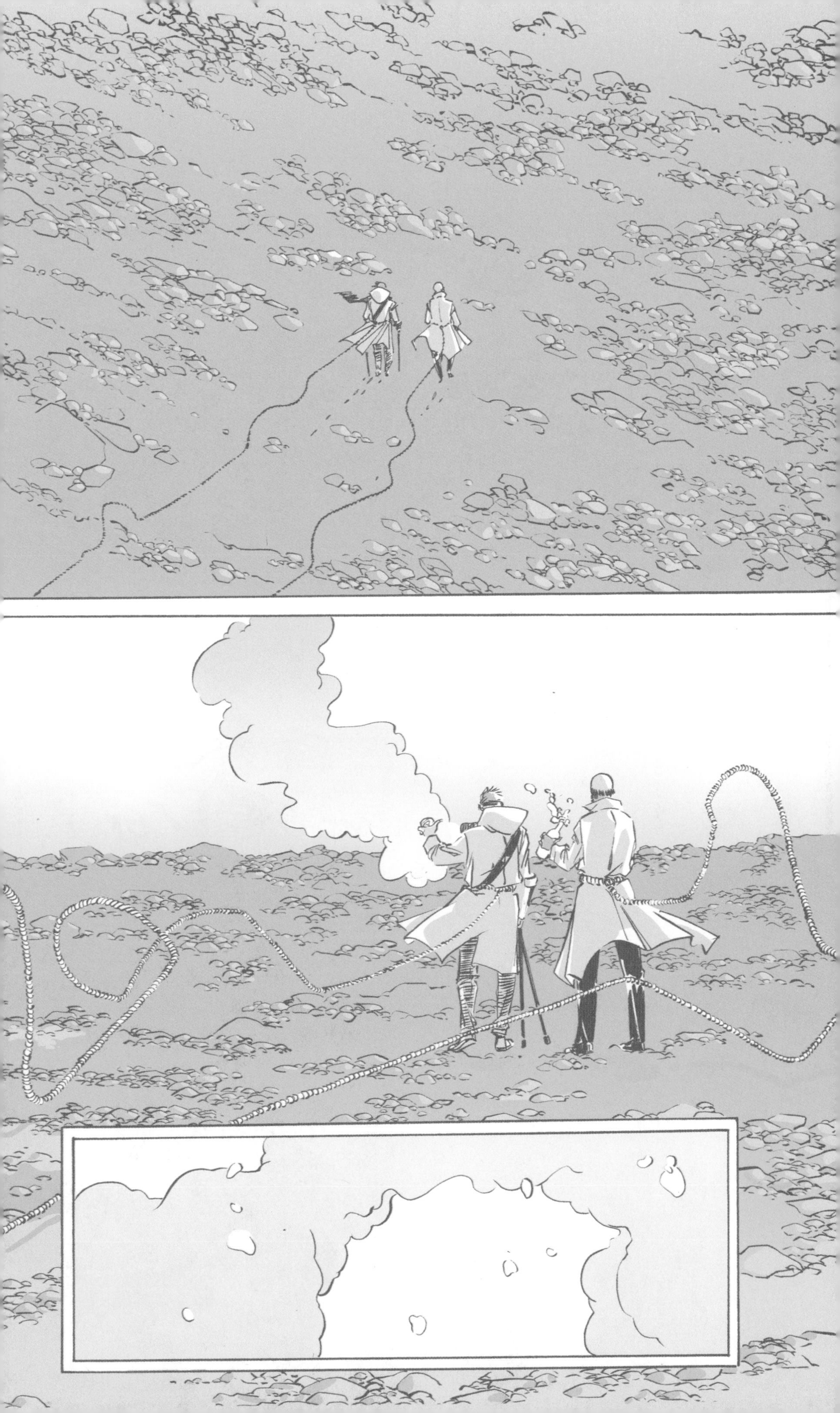

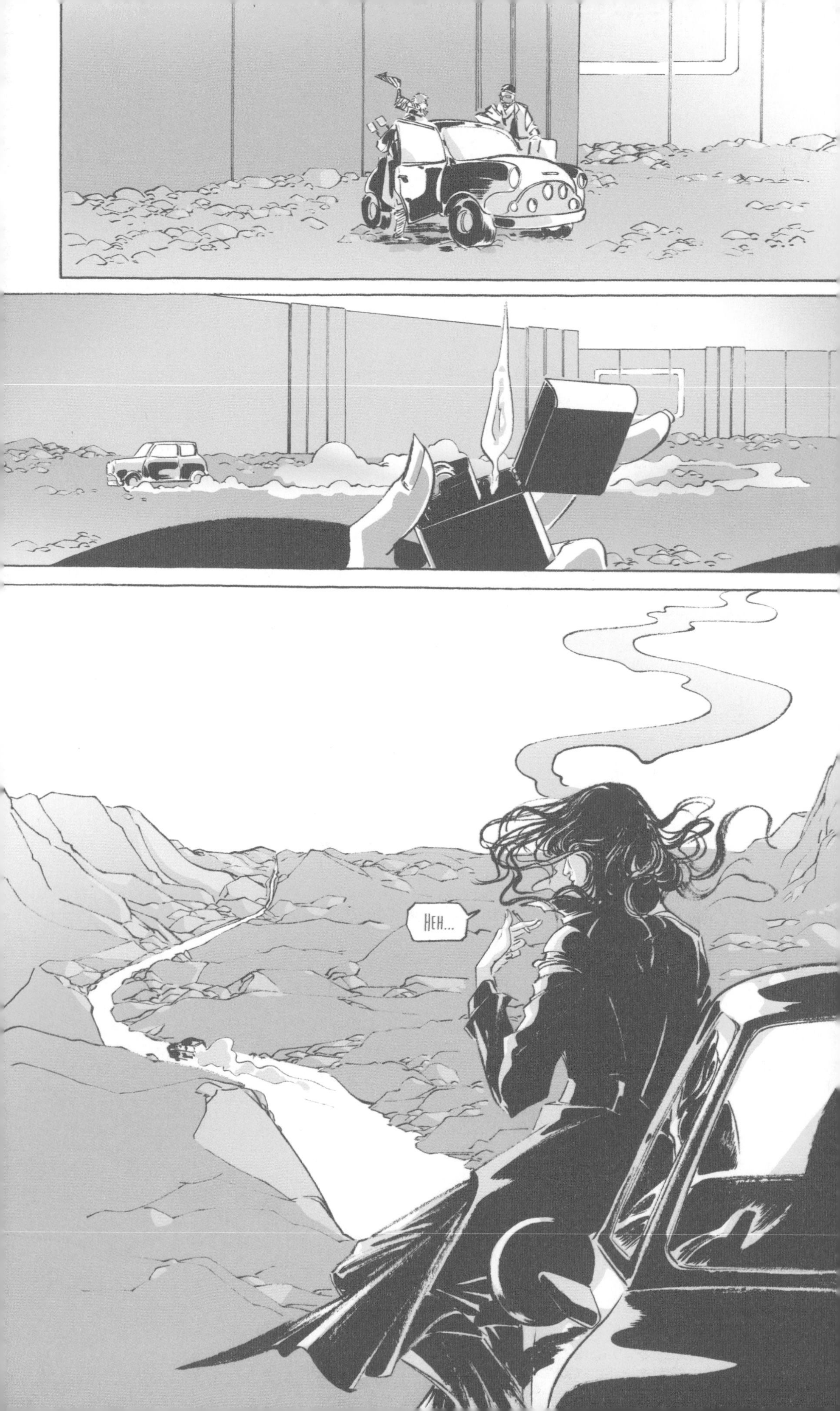
HEH...

THE END.

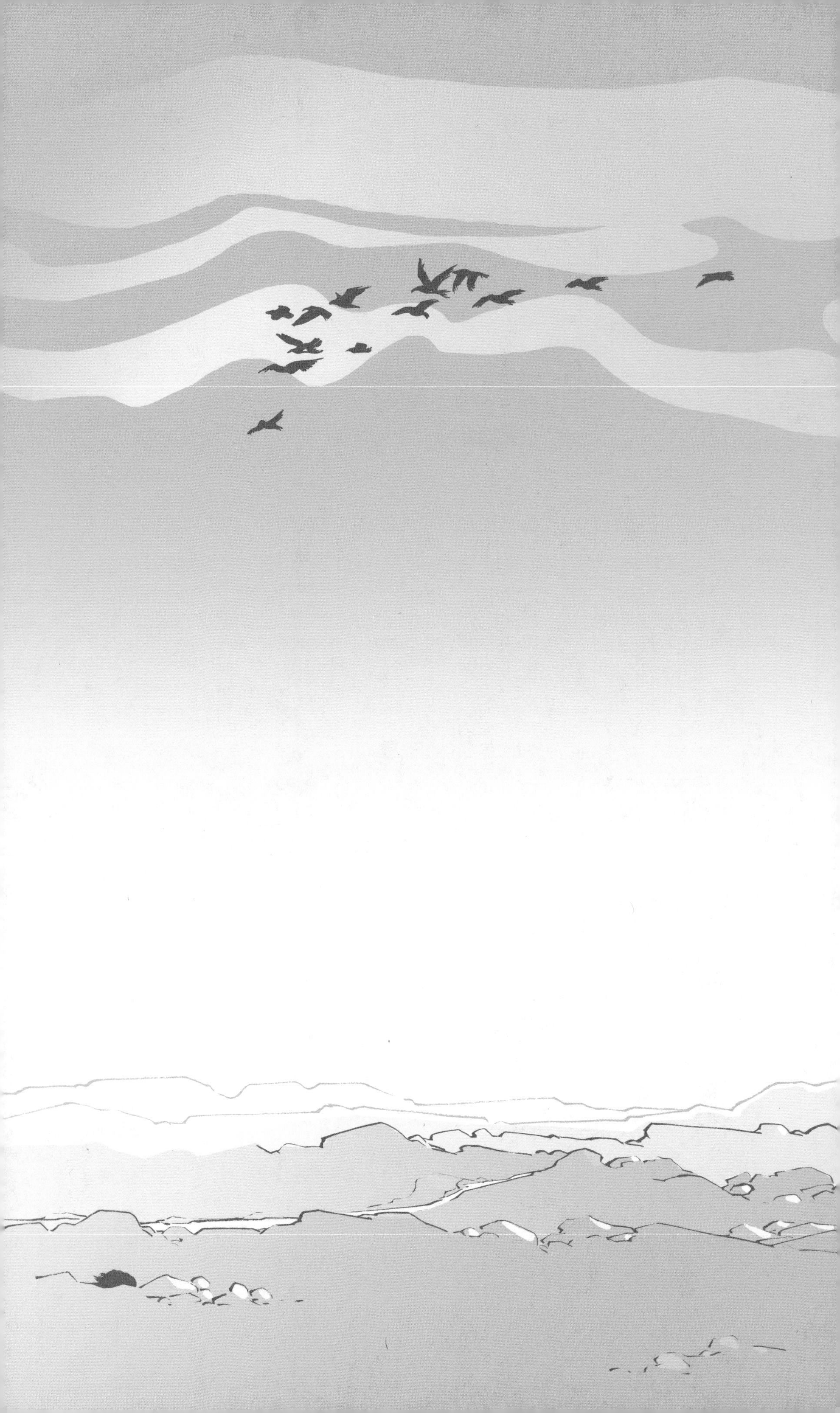

To the ISLAND MAGAZINE and to my brother Brandon Graham for being the most precious home for this story. May this weird insular creature long live forever.

To Miguel Alberte Woodward MD / consultant neurologist for his technical assistance and much appreciated commentary.

To Roque Romero for being the best friend always, and for having helped me doing flats on pages 44-47 and 58-60.

To Michael Bround for the opsin.

To David Brothers, TJ, David Fernández, Marcial Carballido, Javier Peteiro, Victoria Folguiera and Kelly Sue DeConnick for encouraging me with your words.

And to you, friendly Conscience who is reading this,

THANK YOU.

Stitching (an) I.D. Together

ART BY EMMA RÍOS
WORDS BY MIGUEL ALBERTE WOODWARD
DESIGN BY ADDISON DUKE

> "MY BODY IS A CAGE THAT KEEPS ME
> FROM DANCING WITH THE ONE I LOVE
> BUT MY MIND HOLDS THE KEY"
> —FROM ARCADE FIRE'S *MY BODY IS A CAGE.*

Around the spring of 2015 the sensationalist-thirsty media were paying (some) attention to the announcement by an Italian neurosurgeon of his intentions to subject a patient with an incurable neurodegenerative disease to the first head transplant (technically, cephalosomatic anastomosis). As things go, either for news regarding advances of mankind, reporting misfortunes or even – and fortunately- those echoing nonsense, the media's spotlight eventually moves on. Anyhow, by then Emma and I had already been working for over two years in her project I.D. Just to make it clear, no inspiration was drawn from such solemn announcements.

What Emma requested were the technicalities behind the process of changing the carcass, while retaining the soul. Not a clean and elegant method where some nano-robots build a new nervous system from scratch by replicating the original one which you then have to figure out what to do with, but rather a complex surgery with a trade-off between leaving the comforts of home and making the strenuous journey of meeting one's

urge, however founded or powerful, to change body. Setting aside "personal" reasons, there might be a handful of medical conditions where a brain transplant would be considered an option, should the technology be developed some day.

While there is generalized consensus within the scientific community to reject the cloning of complete human beings, the development of a means to create individual organs genetically identical to the host from embryos—or stem cells, alternatively—seems well within reach, if not already in practice with the grafting of relatively "simple" structures such as an engineered trachea or ear. The availability of such organs will revolutionize transplantation medicine chiefly by sparing the immunosuppression and levelling the disparity between recipients and donors, and would not justify a brain transplant.

Other medical advances which are not probably far-reached either include fully understanding and

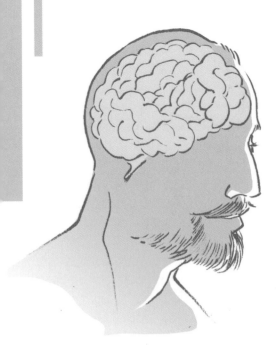

interfering with the molecular pathways that cause even the most aggressive types of cancer, so even an extensive metastatic disease would have a better treatment than resorting to change the whole body—assuming the cancer itself hadn't spread into the brain either. The same would apply both to inborn errors of metabolism and storage disorders as Gaucher's, with abnormal accumulation of compounds throughout the body and which already today enjoy (crude) replacement treatments, or to progressive and fatal myopathies such as Duchenne's.

Hopefully the knowledge of the molecular pathways should also be useful to halt or even reverse the course of neurodegenerative diseases, including the ominous amyotrophic lateral sclerosis or the equally devastating Huntington's disease with its deterministic progression. Plus, the pathological basis of these diseases is a damage to key parts of the brain, so a transplant into a new body would not be likely to solve the issue.

Should these forecasts be true, they would imply that by the time the technology enabling a brain transplant were developed, there should be few "endogenous" somatic illnesses that could not be addressed but with a brain transplant. A possible scenario where it would be considered, could be extensive trauma that makes surgical repair unviable, yet allows for adequate hemodynamic stability in order to extract an undamaged brain.

Whilst the medical indications of a brain transplant would clearly be a concern, a much more heated debate would stir up around the ethical and psychosocial issues. Various solid organ transplants have been successfully performed for over 50 years, hand transplants since the end of the 90s, and face transplants since the mid-2000s. Each of these modalities have required overcoming multiple technical hurdles, such as the need for immunosuppression, the surgical procedure itself, diagnosing brain death or inventing specific devices, as is extracorporeal circulation. Yet they have also brought up ethical questions, of a generic nature such as the process of organ allocation or non-kin living donors, or more specific to the procedure itself, as occurs with transplantation of reproductive tissue.

Arguably, these concerns reached their height when it became a possibility to 'wear someone else's face', following facial transplant, a procedure that has been carried out some 30 times so far. As soon as facial transplant recipients started to come before the cameras, it became clear that any possible resemblance to the donor would be a mere coincidence, and that the fears had been unnecessarily inflated. The transplanted tissues barely did, if at all, carry along the physical traits. Nevertheless, it constitutes a relevant precedent, as the question would quickly make it back to public opinion, should brain transplants be at least feasible. Indeed, it would be profoundly disturbing to even engage in a mere conversation with an old acquaintance that happens not to be the same person anymore. There would likely be some kind of external stigma such as surgery scars due to the opening of the skull, though it probably wouldn't be that difficult to disguise, if not to technically prevent or treat during the operation itself. What would clearly be apparent would be some kind of sequel in any combination of different neurological systems, such as the senses, including sight and hearing, mobility, coordination, speech and swallowing or eye movements, for instance. Even controlling bowel, bladder and sexual function would be an issue. Though the sonority of individual isolated phonemes would probably remain the same as that of the donor's, the articulation of speech would be somehow impaired, and the contents of the discourse be obviously determined by the newly installed brain. Unlike other neurological diseases, the domains that should remain intact would be memory, reasoning and in general all of which are known as higher cerebral functions, as well as mood and personality traits.

Even in the best of cases, some degree of neurological disability might end up giving away the secret for anyone acquainted to the donor. Or at least raising the question of whether the abnormalities are the product of a natural disease, or some kind of intervention. But despite these more or less subtle changes, law enforcement would have a hard time identifying subjects that have had their brain transplanted into another body. Existing biometric parameters, such as fingerprints, iris or retinal scan or the pattern of blood vessels rely solely on characteristics of the donor, and do not provide a means to identify the brain. While it may be technically feasible to distinguish one brain from another by means of some kind of scanner, it is impractical to say least to have a registry of all of the population even if the devices shrank to a fraction of their current size, plus the fact that whatever signature were defined by imaging would probably deteriorate over time, unlike what happens with fingerprints (except in cases of deliberate manipulation). Voice pattern recognition would be a tricky task (see above). A cumbersome and relatively invasive method could rely on performing spinal taps and testing the DNA, which in the case of a brain transplant might reveal a combination of sequences from donor and recipient.

Although the story in I.D. focuses on the microscopic aspects of the surgery, succeeding in achieving the macroscopic part is no minor feat. Through a process of almost obscene simplification, one might find some physical resemblance between a nut and the brain with its hemispheres, gyri and sulci (the parenchyma). The nut's shell also reminds of the skull with the rigid dura mater lining the inside and also dividing the cranial cavity in sections, as are the anterior, middle and posterior fossae, or the left and right cerebral hemispheres. Again, overtly simplifying the process, the surgery would be a bit like separating the shell from the nut, without harming neither the recipient's parenchyma nor the donor's lining. To complicate things further, there are a number of vessels traversing the millimetric space that separates brain and dura, some of which may be sacrificed whilst others would have to be appropriately joined together afterwards between graft and host. The twelve pairs of cranial nerves, serving multiple critical functions including sight, eye movements, hearing and facial movement, follow awkward routes to find their way out of the skull, and would need to be severed ant then matched again. The four main vessels (two large and anterior—the internal carotid arteries—and two smaller

and posterior—the vertebral arteries) that ascend from the neck, enter the skull and provide the blood supply to the brain, among the few anatomical structures with barely any variation between individuals, would require detaching probably at the base of the skull, before they gave any branches, in a region of difficult access.

To date, the largest piece of skull that is removed during neurosurgery is performed during decompressive craniectomy, in which well less than half of the cranial vault is exposed. This is mainly due to basic principle of avoiding any damage to the dural sinuses, large veins included within the dura mater and just beneath the bone, two of which run front to back in the midline of the head, others in the hindhead. As the manipulation of the whole brain and all of the processes described in the preceding paragraph would be impossible through such a small opening, some kind of method would have to be devised to reconstruct the sinuses and ensure their perviousness after the surgery.

Unlike thoracic, abdominal or pelvic surgeries, which have enjoyed enormous advances with the advent of key-hole surgery and even robotic suites to assist surgeons in their tasks, neurosurgery has barely ever benefited so far from such devices. Probably the only way to tackle the difficulties exposed above, with areas in the base of

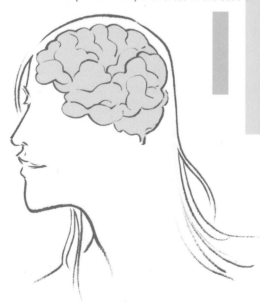

the skull of very dire access to conventional instruments, would require the development of minimally invasive and probably flexible robotical systems to find their way to such regions.

Yet the description of the technique in I.D. focuses mainly

on an even more ambitious stage of the process: the one that happens at a cellular level, once all the visible stitching together has happened. Functional magnetic resonance imaging (fMRI) has already achieved remarkable feats in further understanding the areas and tracts involved in specific neural processes. With further refinements of the technique and improvements in resolution, it is likely it will allow in the near future for a precise—and, most importantly, individualized—mapping of the ascending and descending pathways in the spinal cord, particularly at the proposed site of the splicing with the brain, the area known as the craneocervical junction.

As may be inferred from the above stated, one of the findings of such mappings will be that humans do not share a common interface, unlike a USB connection with four matching pins at each end. Actually, diversity is one of the hallmarks of living beings. Thus, although there is a general pattern governing the arrangement the bundles of nerve fibres in the spinal cord, assuming graft and donor's neurons do fuse, it is not unlikely an impulse coming from the primary motor cortex in the brain and signalling the flexion of the right elbow ends up finally causing a flexion of the right index finger, for instance. Hence the need for rehabilitation to regain control of movements, and the expectations of, at best, a sub-optimal motor and sensory recovery.

To promote the fusing of both ends of the long output fibres that neurons sprout, which are formally named axons, we proposed a system for a sort of biological 'staining' of each basic neuronal type: motor, sensitive and autonomic cells. An engineered neurotropic virus specific for each of these types would infect them, both in host and donor, and it would contain a wavelength specific light-sensitive protein that would attach itself to the microtubules that constitute the scaffolding of the axons. Allowing ourselves (yet another) artistic license, we devised a method in which two incredibly precise laser beams would induce changes in the very place they met, but leave unharmed any tissues they moved through. Such changes would imply activating the opsins or light-sensitive proteins to provoke the redirection of the axons towards their matching stump on the other side, thus inducing fusion of the fibres. This technique, named optogenetics, is already being used in animal experiments in which light beams are able to modulate in vivo the behaviour of different

parts of the guinea pig. There may be a possibility this technology is one day used in surgeries far more modest than a brain transplant, such as repairing a damaged spinal cord or treating some types of blindness. Or maybe it's stem cells the ones that finally get these jobs done.

By now, the reader is likely aware that the chances of the whole process we have devised for I.D. to become reality, and brain transplants actually occur, are rather meagre. It is an extravagance; an imaginary process we have come up with in the attempt of giving scientific grounds to an entirely fictional story. Not only should we reckon it, we might as well finish this dissertation with the grandiloquent announcement we started it with, and which can be deflated to a bluff, a bunch of methods with no experimental background to support them, despising the basic principles of neuroscience. Whether or not they get on a TED stage, the old piece of advice is still in force: beware of false prophets.

MIGUEL ALBERTE WOODWARD, MD.
@MIGUELAWOODWARD

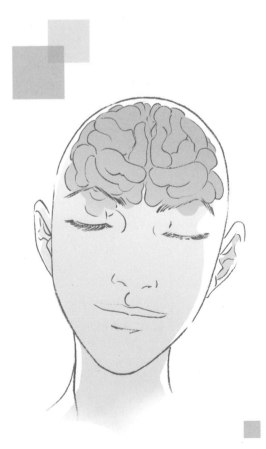

Emma Ríos Maneiro

Emma is a cartoonist based in Spain. She shifted her focus to a mix of both architecture and small press until working on comics full time in 2007. Having worked for Boom! Studios and Marvel, she returns to creator-owned production in 2013 thanks to Image Comics. She currently co-edits the ISLAND magazine with Brandon Graham, and co-creates PRETTY DEADLY with Kelly Sue DeConnick and MIRROR with Hwei Lim.

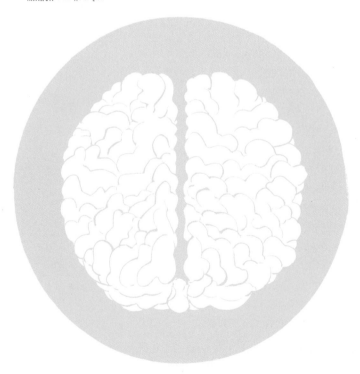

Miguel Alberte Woodward

Miguel once as a kid couldn't help but watch a rather disgusting documentary showing the parts of an animal's brain. Either that, or it was the family tradition of headaches that needed something doing. One thing led to another, and eventually he came to make a living as a neurologist for the public health system of Galicia, Spain. More accustomed to tormenting a specialized public with an arid, technical prose, he seized the opportunity I.D. offered to write his first paper addressing the general public. If one thing he knows about scientific advising, is that it's gone missing in the average TV medical drama.

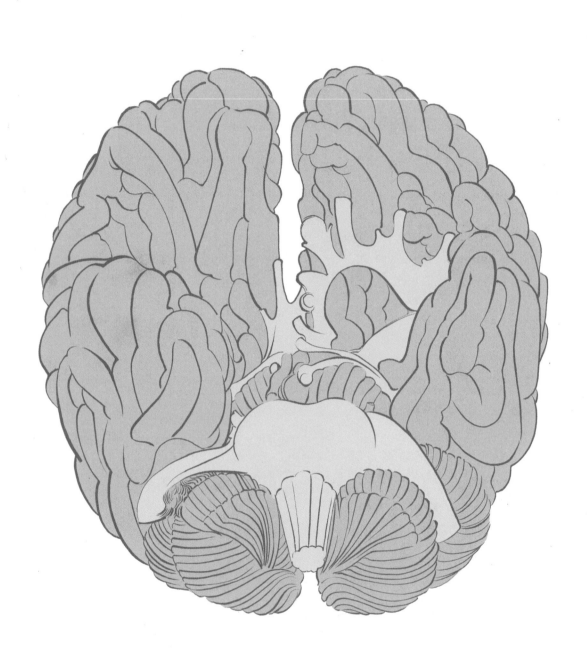

Robert Kirkman – Chief Operating Officer
Erik Larsen – Chief Financial Officer
Todd McFarlane – President
Marc Silvestri – Chief Executive Officer
Jim Valentino – Vice-President

Eric Stephenson – Publisher
Corey Murphy – Director of Sales
Jeff Boison – Director of Publishing Planning & Book Trade Sales
Jeremy Sullivan – Director of Digital Sales
Kat Salazar – Director of PR & Marketing

Emily Miller – Director of Operations
Branwyn Bigglestone – Senior Accounts Manager
Sarah Mello – Accounts Manager
Drew Gill – Art Director
Jonathan Chan – Production Manager

Meredith Wallace – Print Manager
Briah Skelly – Publicity Assistant
Sasha Head – Sales & Marketing Production Designer
Randy Okamura – Digital Production Designer
David Brothers – Branding Manager

Ally Power – Content Manager
Addison Duke – Production Artist
Vincent Kukua – Production Artist
Tricia Ramos – Production Artist
Jeff Stang – Direct Market Sales Representative
Emilio Bautista – Digital Sales Associate
Leanna Caunter – Accounting Assistant
Chloe Ramos-Peterson – Administrative Assistant

IMAGECOMICS.COM

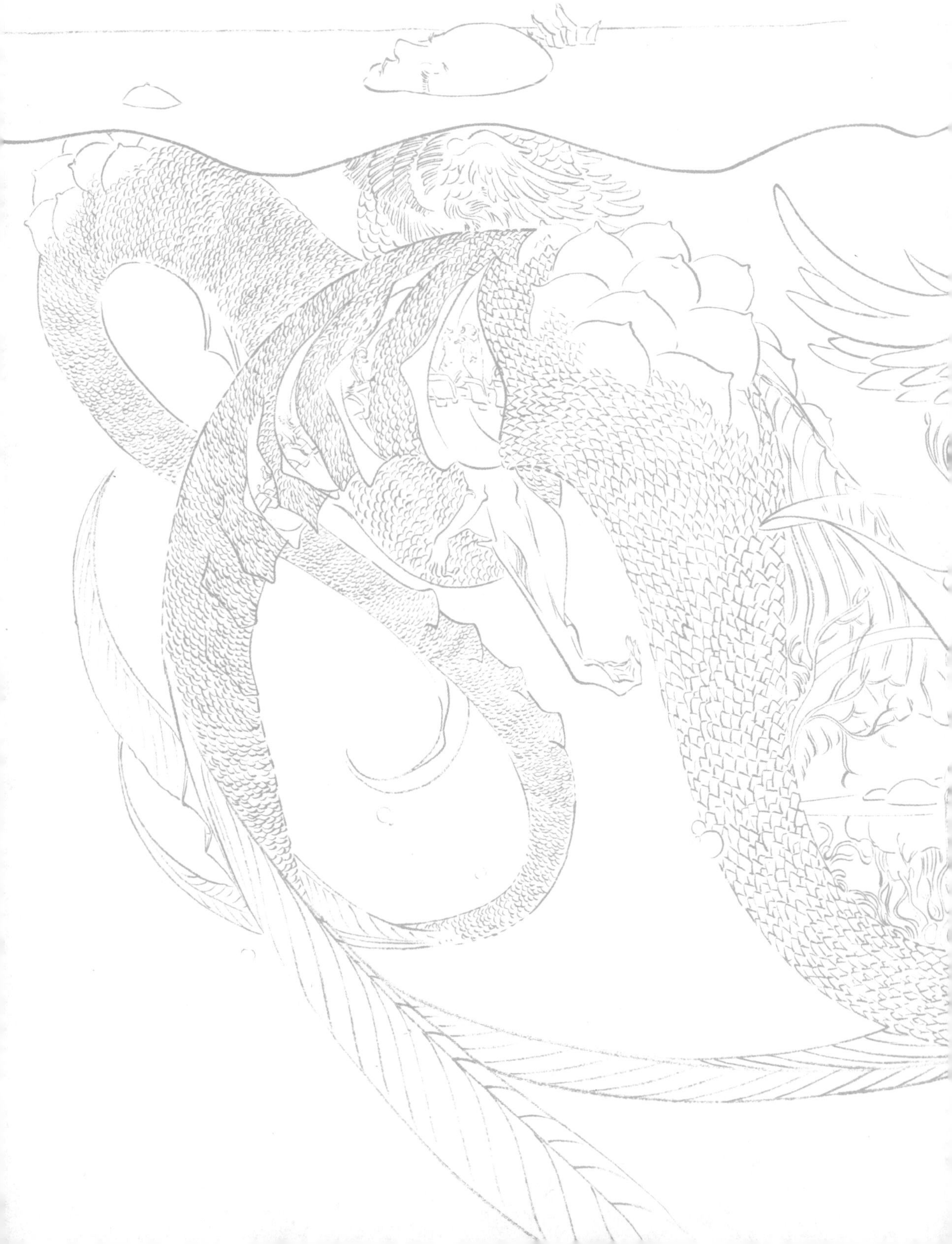

I.D. was originally published in the pages of the Island magazine by Image Comics.
https://imagecomics.com/comics/series/island

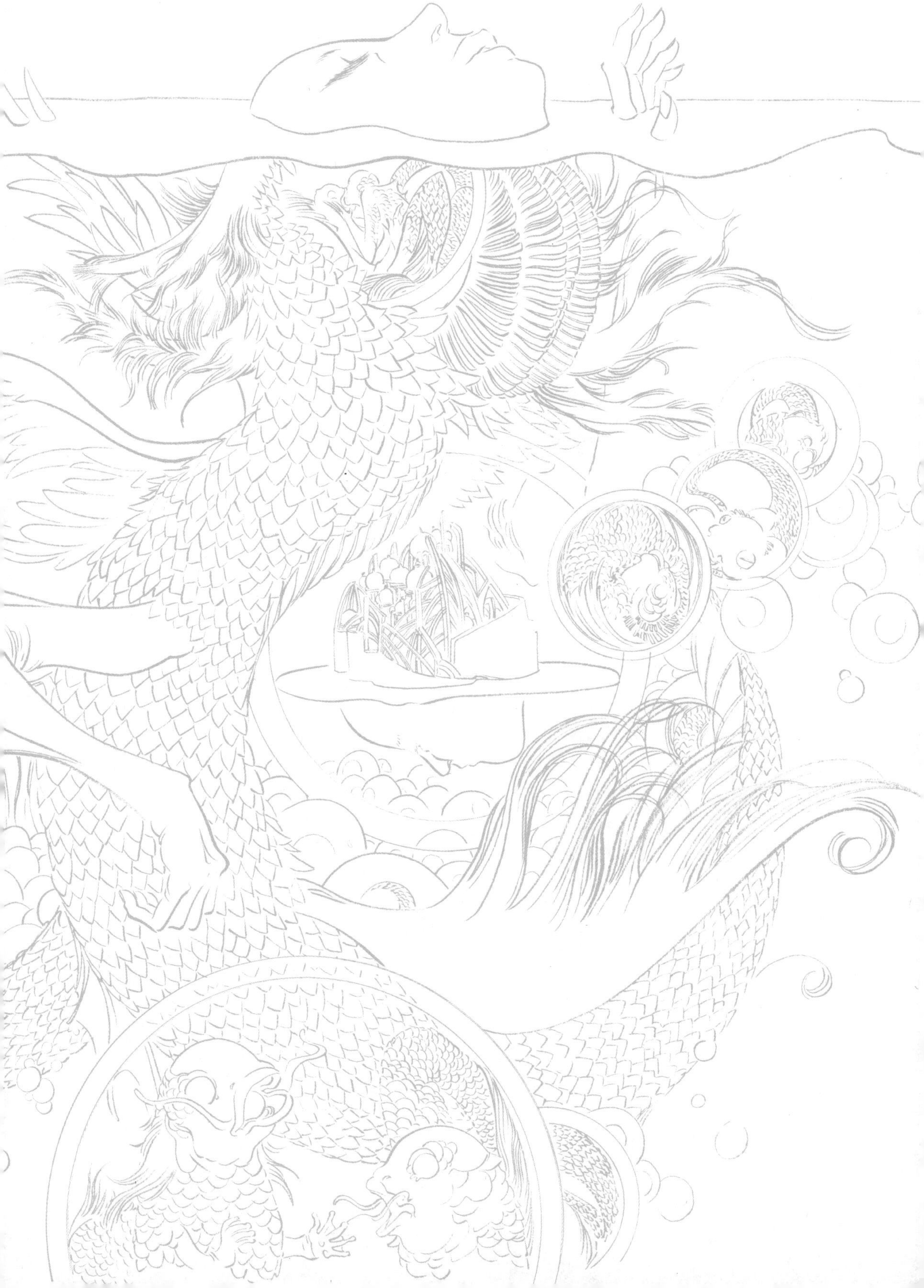

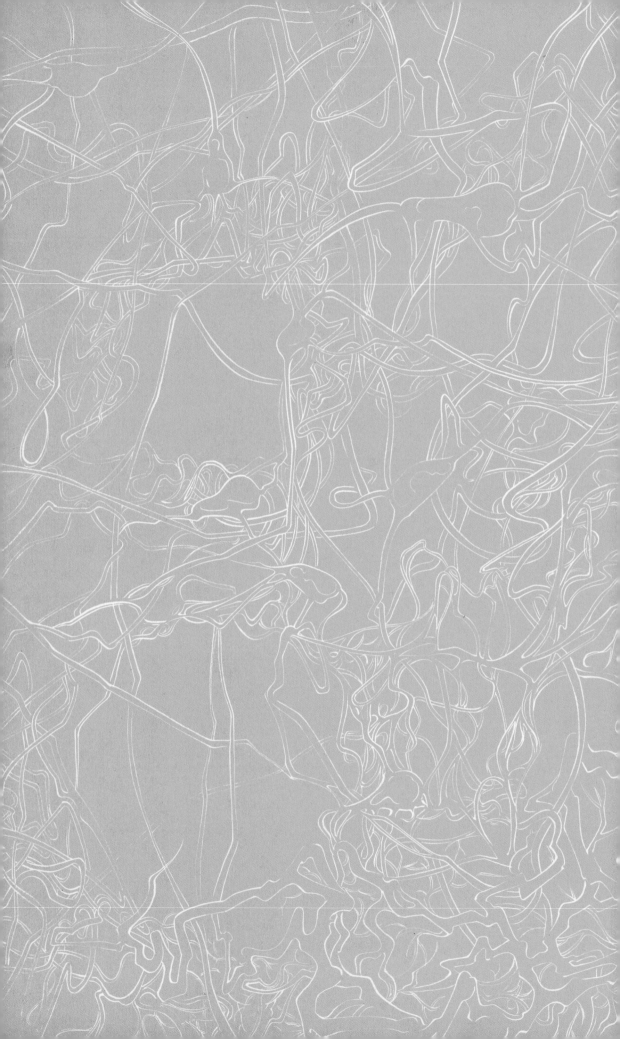